# THE
# HOARDERS

## JEAN STRINGAM

ISBN 13: 978-1-59955-407-5

Published by Bonneville Books, an imprint of Cedar Fort, Inc.,
2373 W. 700 S., Springville, UT 84663
Distributed by Cedar Fort, Inc., www.cedarfort.com

LIBRARY OF CONGRESS CATALOGING-IN-PUBLICATION DATA

Stringam, Jean, 1945-
  The hoarders / Jean Stringam.
    p. cm.
  Summary: Two boys in a dysfunctional family lean on each other to survive, including hoarding food and supplies so they will have food when their mother doesn't feed them.
  ISBN 978-1-59955-407-5
  1. Dysfunctional families--Fiction. 2. Teenage boys--Fiction. 3. Domestic fiction, American. I. Title.

  PS3619.T7527H63 2010
  813'.6--dc22

              2010008732

Cover design by Megan Whittier
Cover design © 2010 by Lyle Mortimer
Edited and typeset by Heidi Doxey

Printed in the United States of America

10 9 8 7 6 5 4 3 2 1

Printed on acid-free paper

# DEDICATED

To the wonderful MOBS,
with my love always:

Sarah, Julian, Virginia, and Gabriel

Benjamin, Suzanne, Aidan, and Zoe

Hannah Jean

Laura, Dakota, and Jerako

Jessica, Aaron, and Ezra

# ACKNOWLEDGMENTS

I'd like to thank all the dedicated staff at Cedar Fort, including Jennifer Fielding for plucking this book out of the slush pile, Heidi Doxey for seeing the text afresh, and Sheralyn Pratt for getting it out there.

To my wonderful readers of multiple early drafts, Linda Benson, Hannah Beesley, Jessica Seibert, and Sarah Mogzec, I feel a huge debt of gratitude. I'm also very grateful for the perspectives of excellent readers such as Cherri Jones, Kathleen Taylor, Jennie Kallunki, and Nancy Jensen. My sincere thanks to each of you for your gifts of time and expertise.

A special thank you goes to Aidan for the worm joke and to all my young friends who gave me advice about their favorite jokes.

The debt I owe my parents, Bryce and Mary Stringam, for their legacy of the love of books and learning, I must simply pass on to the next generations.

# CONTENTS

# Contents

# ONE
# MUDDY WALK

M y brother, Joaquin, and I are hiding out. Nobody knows where we live, and that's how we want it. If anybody finds out that Joaquin and I have moved back into the summer cottage with Aunt Amy like she is, we might have to go live with strangers. We need to stay with her no matter what. No way am I going to let strangers take her. Besides, two brothers might get split up between two families. Joaquin needs me and so does Aunt Amy, so I'm going to make sure nobody ever knows we live here.

I'll bet the school reported us missing while we were in the hospital keeping watch on Aunt Amy. If the police had come here to do a house-check, they'd have found that this little house, belonging to Aunt Amy and her brothers, stayed empty for over a month. That ought to discourage anybody from nosing around, even Dead Uncle Dick.

Joaquin and I watch the houses around the lake like two sight dogs. Right now it's starting to be spring, but it's still

1

cold and wet outside and the people haven't begun opening up their vacation homes yet. That's good and bad. Good
because we don't have to worry about nosy questions. Bad
because we've almost eaten up all the food in the summer
cottage as well as the food hoard we keep in our backpacks
in the bottom of our closet.

It's also bad because both Aunt Amy's and our money
is almost gone. We need to pick up some odd jobs that pay,
but we can't wait for when people start to move back into the
houses for the summer. We need food right now. You might
say we're in a tight spot.

Aunt Amy is the grown-up we live with, and she needs
us. She used to be smart and pretty and funny, but when she
finally woke up in the hospital, she had changed. She has her
head bandages off, but she doesn't laugh anymore and she
keeps saying really weird stuff.

This summer cottage by the lake has two big rooms. One
is a living room and kitchen with a great big fireplace. The
other is a bedroom with a big bed for Aunt Amy and a set
of bunk beds where Joaquin and I sleep. We both prefer the
top bunk because it's by a high window where we can look
outside. We take turns.

It's my turn, so I'm sitting on the top bunk, looking out
the window, when I hear Joaquin calling me. "Cheyenne!
Come here! Aunt Amy is trying to get out!"

"Hold the door shut!"

"I am!"

I scramble off the bed and down the post. Joaquin is
holding onto the doorknob with both hands, and Aunt Amy

is pulling hard on his arms. I know she is much stronger than both of us together, so I pull a kitchen chair very close to them and stand on it. I might get knocked over, but she might take notice of me. She stops struggling with Joaquin and looks at me, one eye up and out from where it should be focusing. The other one's okay.

"Aunt Amy, what do you want?" I ask her. I already know she wants outside, but after the operation we heard the hospital doctors say she needed practice with speaking. She's forgotten a lot of the words she used to know. I didn't know that was possible. You wake up after being unconscious in the hospital for a few weeks and you can't remember words anymore? That's got to be one of the scariest things I've ever heard of. About as scary as Dead Uncle Dick.

Not having all her words makes Aunt Amy very frustrated. I'm trying to get her to express what she's thinking. I was in fifth grade before we quit school and that was part of our writing assignments: expressive communication, the teacher said. Joaquin is supposed to be in first grade. I have him read to me a lot, so he shouldn't be too behind if we ever start going to school again—which I don't think we will.

"Aunt Amy, tell me what you want!" I shout at her to get her attention.

She looks a little offended because I shouted at her. She drops Joaquin's arm and thinks for a minute. "Go outside," she says. "Now."

Joaquin shakes his head at her and looks fierce.

I tell him, "I think we should take her for a walk, Joaquin. The doctor said she needed to get lots of rest and exercise.

This house is too small for her to get any exercise. I'll keep her here while you get all our coats."

I coax Aunt Amy to put on her coat. Then I push her gently onto the chair that I was standing on so I can pull her boots up and tie them. It's really muddy outside.

Joaquin opens the door, and we each try to take one of her hands. She won't let us, though. At first Aunt Amy grabs the sides of her big skirt and swishes them from side to side with each step, but she tires very quickly and settles down. After we've gone past the big yards of about six houses she starts to slow way down, so I try to turn her around to go home, but she won't turn.

She shouts, "More! More!" and busts out walking with more energy. Joaquin and I trot to keep up.

We've gone past about twelve houses when she completely stops. "I'm tired," she says. "Too tired. Can't go on." She starts to sit down on the ground in the mud.

I yell for Joaquin to push up on her bum from behind so she can't sit down. If she sits down we might never get her up again. She was sort of like dead in the hospital for two weeks before she woke up. I'm really scared that if she gets wet and cold in the mud that she could get sick enough to die. We've got to get her home and dried off.

I turn her around and Joaquin pushes on her bum for all he's worth. She's a lot taller than us, and it's hard to get her moving. I pull on her arms as hard as I can, and she starts to walk, all slow and trudgey. Only two more houses to go.

And then Joaquin slips—falls flat on his face in the mud. He's soaking wet and wants to cry. But when you're in this much trouble, the fact is even little guys know the point where you can't cry. He picks himself up.

Aunt Amy is very interested in looking at him. "Joaquin is dirty," she says.

"Very dirty and wet and cold," Joaquin says, his cheeks trembling.

She takes her clean fingers and carefully tries to wipe off his muddy face, just like she used to do mine when I was little. She wipes her muddy fingers clean on her skirt.

I remember the good times when we were safe with Aunt Amy and I want to sit down in the mud and cry. Everybody is feeling the same way. Aunty Amy is whimpering, "I'm too tired. I can't go on."

Joaquin starts to push again and I start to pull, but Aunt Amy keeps on wailing in a voice she never used to use before. "I'm too tired. I don't care. Let me sit here. Go to sleep. I want to sleep and die right here. It's too far. I'm too tired."

If she'd just take normal steps we'd be fine. Joaquin and I don't let go. We've got to get her home.

We're almost at the doorway when she seems to recognize it. She stops pulling against us and walks by herself into the house, all slow and draggy. I get her to sit down on the chair so I can pull off her muddy skirt. Joaquin knows how to take care of himself.

I guess you could say Joaquin and I are in a pile of trouble. I sure wish I could tell you how we're going to get ourselves out of this, but I don't see a way yet. All I can tell you is how we got here. I'll start kind of close to the beginning.

# TWO

# SIGHT DOGS

I have the handicap of a strange name. It looks just fine when you read it on paper, but when you hear it aloud, it makes some kids think they can punch you. Cheyenne. See what I mean? Written down, you can tell it's the name of an old-time Indian warrior and a modern town in Wyoming. But when you say it aloud it comes out, "shy Ann."

Once I asked Momma why she did that to me and she told me how, just before I was born, she was driving back home to live with her parents and got side-tracked in Cheyenne, Wyoming. She thought it was a wonderful name with a beautiful sound. "Like wind and sunlight in the trees," she said.

My teacher said that in the old days Native American children's names changed as they grew up. How they handled problems created the person they became. The name they carried would change to follow the path of who they were becoming. I really like that idea.

My grandpa's favorite singer had a hit song called "A Boy Named Sue." Grandpa would sing it to me sometimes. His eyes would twinkle and Momma would yell at him, but he made it like it was our private joke. That was way before school started, though. It turned out Grandpa was kind of warning me about what was to come.

Maybe Momma just didn't have skills for naming boys, because she got it wrong twice. She gave my little brother a name that sounds like an action word, a verb. Joaquin. Sounds just like "walking." I asked my mother why she chose that name and she said because it was mysterious and exciting. Anybody named Joaquin would have to be full of imagination and energy. My little brother is all of that, but I can't see that the name did it for him.

I think my mother has the most beautiful name in the world. Coco. I've said it over and over a million times and it's still the loveliest name I can imagine. To simplify things Momma gave us her own last name, Walker, the same as Grandpa and Grandma. But it complicates our name problems. That makes me "shy Ann walker" and my brother "walking walker."

One of Momma's ex-boyfriends (the one with green cowboy boots and yellow nose hairs) would just about burst from laughing every time we'd come in the room. "Here comes the walking walker. Har, har, har!" Somebody would call and ask for my mom, and he'd say, "She's out walking shy Ann. Har, har, har. Naw, she's right here. I'll get her." He never got over the jokes.

That's the thing about a strange name. All your life people

keep discovering it. You have to listen to the same jokes over and over again until pretty soon you start sorting people by whether they laugh aloud or just think the laugh.

I've done two things about my name problem. I have a private place in my mind where I keep all the images of what my name really means. I started with what Momma said, "Cheyenne: the sound of wind and sunlight in the trees." Then I added the ideas, "Cheyenne: brave, fast legs, solves problems, whippet."

Another thing I did when I got tired of all the name jokes—I gave myself another name. I taught Joaquin how to rename himself, and we've both been doing it for years. We are very careful not to tell any adults, though, because it makes them feel uneasy. We almost told Aunt Amy once, but that was before she had her big change.

I've learned a few things that I aim to teach Joaquin. The first big one is this: the reason kids don't get what they want is because they waste their focus. Kids need to be like sight dogs: greyhounds and afghans and whippets. These dogs lock their eyes on their prey (maybe a rabbit) and never let their view waver. That's how I watch grown-ups.

Just before I was born Momma moved back home so her mother and father could take care of us. I don't think I had any sight-dog skills when we lived with my grandparents. I was little then, anyway. But my grandpa died when I was four and that changed things for Momma.

When somebody dies, all their stuff is lumped together and called an estate. When Grandpa died, Aunt Amy says half of Momma's share of the estate went into a special bank account for me and any brothers or sisters I might eventually have, but Momma got to take the rest of the money and do anything she wanted with it. Aunt Amy says Grandma had lots of advice about how Momma should spend the money: get an education, start a business, leave it in the bank. That was too much advice for Momma.

She wanted Las Vegas.

No kidding. Las Vegas. We moved from my grandparents' lake home with cool breezes in the trees and sunshine and birds and water everywhere, to the top of a steel hotel in the middle of a sizzling-hot city. I remember how the city lights looked at night, so sparkling and beautiful it made me sigh inside.

I remember taking trips up an elevator where I could see out over the city. I thought palm trees were a wonderful idea and wished I could be a monkey. Then I'd be able to play and sleep right beside my food.

We ate in restaurants every day. If I didn't like the food, I could ask for something else and get it. Momma didn't make me eat anything I didn't like. She'd smile at her boyfriend and say, "Life's too short to spend it unhappy."

Every night Momma would tuck me into bed, kiss me good night, and tell me to go to sleep. Then the doorbell would ring and I'd hear a man's voice. Momma would laugh, then he'd laugh, and then there'd be the sound of the door closing. If I tried to stay awake until she came home, I'd be alone in the bedroom for a long time. Usually I went to sleep.

I remember how people at the hotel would ask us, "And

who's this little man?" After a few months people in the elevators who recognized me would say, "Hello, Little Man." I thought it was my name and called myself Little Man.

One of Momma's boyfriends (the one with white canvass shoes and a glittering gold watch) called himself by his initials. He was quite respectful of my name, Cheyenne Walker, so I began to think it was cool to call myself by my initials too. But I never used my real initials of CW. I told everyone to call me LM, but I didn't tell anybody that it stood for Little Man. As it turned out, that boyfriend was mostly respectful of Momma's money. Until it ran out.

After a year in Las Vegas, Momma called Aunt Amy to come and help us move. They yelled at each other the whole time because Momma had used up all her money.

I remember Momma yelling, "I did things, and I saw things, and I met people. For once in my whole life I got to live like I wanted to!"

Aunt Amy said, "You should have spent it on a high school diploma."

Momma was packing my clothes and began to throw them at Aunt Amy. Listening to them fight was hard, but all these colors and shapes flying through the air were interesting to watch. I did my best to be a sight dog on them.

"You made me do it!" Momma yelled. Yellow T-shirt.

"What are you talking about?" Brown bear slippers.

"Leaving school after tenth grade! Going on road trips with our guitars! Singing on sidewalks for money!" A whole drawer full of socks, two fistfuls at a time.

"You can't make a person do much of anything they don't

already want to do," Aunt Amy said. Blue-and-white–striped pajamas with grey feet whiz across the room.

"All that hippie stuff was what you loved! Not me! That wasn't me!" Momma yelled, my blue jeans with a hole in one knee flying through the air. I am trying not to feel scared, so I look at the clothes as hard as I can.

"So you quit the life. You made the decision, not me." One grey sneaker with laces.

"You should have taken one of your precious friends." The other grey sneaker without laces.

"You begged me to come." Red summer pajamas with black dragons.

"But you made it sound like so much fun! And it wasn't!" Momma might be about ready to cry. I'm listening to her voice to know. But an orange T-shirt comes toward me like a weird puffy pumpkin and lands on my head.

"You were just dying to leave home. You could hardly wait to get rid of all those restrictions."

Momma slings five shirts still on the plastic hangers.

"Ouch! Stop it! It's a cheap shot to say I made you do it. You wanted to!" Aunt Amy's getting steamed up, irritated. Dark purple sweater with white edging from Grandma Miriam for Christmas. I only wore it once. It was too hot in Las Vegas for a Christmas sweater.

Most of what I know about my mother comes from her fights with Aunt Amy when I concentrated on being a sight dog. I wish I had had longer with Momma. I remember her smell: flowers, summer, warm, soft.

## THREE

# GETTING MONEY

Before Aunt Amy became so sick, she used to say I was way different from any other kid she'd ever met. I asked her how many kids she'd met. Usually grown-ups stop being so nice if you say those sorts of things, but not Aunt Amy. She sat very still on the bed and started to make a list of every kid she'd known since after she'd grown up. It wasn't a very long list, and she included a couple of people I personally know to be adults, but I let her carry her point. I've thought a lot about it and have a theory I'm teaching Joaquin. I think I'm different from all the kids Aunt Amy knows because I know what to want.

It's a good idea to keep the want list short. I tell Joaquin we each get three wants and the first two have to be food and money. Those two are private wants: we don't tell anybody. The third want can be anything, but we have to keep it secret. There's a difference between private and secret. Private is something I share with Joaquin, but secret is what I keep to myself. I've trained my little brother to never tell what his secret third wish is, not even to me. Sometimes he wants to, but I tell him to shush.

Joaquin and I have nearly become experts in wishing. We began by trying to wish on the evening star, the planet Venus. You know how the wish goes: "Star light, star bright, first star I've seen tonight. I wish I may, I wish I might, have the wish I wish tonight." Apparently that's a very potent old-fashioned wish.

Maybe it would work if you were a rich kid at the top of a hotel in the desert like I was in Las Vegas. Or maybe it would work if you were a farm kid or out on an ocean, but it never worked for Joaquin and me. All we could see from our apartment window were taller buildings and street lights. There are lots of pictures of starry nights, so they must happen somewhere. Just not where we lived.

We tried wishing with birthday candles, but we didn't have very many birthdays between us. One year Momma's boyfriend (the one with a gold tooth and the silver belt buckle) put trick candles that didn't blow out on my birthday cake. He thought it was a really funny idea. I guess he could laugh because he had plenty of money and all the food he wanted, so wishes didn't mean a thing to him. That's how I lost my one chance for a really good wish for a whole year.

Other kids said the tooth fairy came to their house and left money. But teeth take a long time to loosen up when you're waiting to get started on a tooth fairy project, and Joaquin was too little to contribute any teeth at all. If there is a real tooth fairy, she hasn't ever shown up at my place. I figure it's probably like the whole Santa Claus business, and Momma wasn't very diligent at either one of them.

We added other wish objects, like the first squeeze of a new tube of toothpaste. And then we added the second squeeze, so Joaquin could get his wish. And days when we needed wishes really bad, we'd add all the squeezes until you started noticing the tube was getting flat. Those wishes were basically unsuccessful. Something good might happen, but it wasn't because of the squeeze on the new tube.

We began thinking we ought to start wishing on weird stuff that usually doesn't come up. Something really distinctive would have power in it, wouldn't you think? Like a wind that takes your book bag right off your back, a goldfish flopping on the side walk, a tree bent over and planted in the ground at both ends. I was certain these kinds of wishes would have a lot of energy behind them, but the opportunity to see weird stuff doesn't come up that often, even when you're very careful to look for it. Then I thought the most powerful thing to wish on would be a dead body. But that was before I saw one.

I spent a lot of time with Aunt Amy after we left Las Vegas because Momma was a bar maid at night and had to sleep during the day. I couldn't go to work with Momma at the bar, she said, but Aunt Amy took me to work with her. She had spent her estate money on a lady's boutique—a store with dresses in beautiful colors, and at least a thousand bottles of perfume. Aunt Amy had found us an apartment near her store, and I liked helping her. I learned how to run the vacuum and how to smile and say "hello" to the ladies.

I really don't understand why people coming into the store always said, "And who's this little man?" It was the same as in the Las Vegas hotel all over again. There's just no good answer to that question. I could have said, "My name is Cheyenne Walker," but that would have started the name jokes, and anyway I didn't think they really wanted to know. If I'd said, "Can I help you?" they'd have asked me for something that I wouldn't be able to get them. And if I'd said, "Aunt Amy is the store owner, so this place is more mine than yours," they'd have reported me to Aunt Amy as a smart-alecky kid. I didn't want to hurt Aunt Amy. She needed the women to like coming to the store.

To be honest, there was another reason I never said a word to them. They probably wouldn't understand what I said anyway. I didn't speak very clearly back then. So whenever people asked me, "And who's this little man?" I'd just smile at them. That was all the information they wanted.

When the customers leaned over to smile down at me, I could look straight into their eyes using my sight-dog eyes. Aunt Amy said I was a big help in the boutique because no shopper wants to put something in her pocket without paying for it when there's a sight dog trained on them.

Aunt Amy would bring lunch for us to eat in the store, but Momma usually didn't think about supper. She didn't need to eat very much, she said. But she forgot that I was a growing boy and needed a lot more food than I was getting. That's when I began my food hoard. I'd take boxes of crackers and cans of food from the cupboard and hide them in my room.

Right about then I started calling myself HM instead of LM. It's not secret anymore, so I can say what the initials meant. They stood for Hungry Man. I've pretty much been hungry ever since we left Las Vegas unless Aunt Amy was visiting. We would sit at the table while she cooked and would smell everything happening on the stove. Aunt Amy said we probably got half our calories just from smelling.

After Momma was gone and we went to live with Aunt Amy, Joaquin even started to get some baby fat, sort of round and soft under his chin and around his tummy. I think it was too late for me. I'm still basically Stick Man, but sometimes when my stomach was full the night before, I noticed that I could run farther and faster on the playground at school.

# FOUR

# BIG STINK

When your room stinks before you even open the door, you know you've got a problem. I learned that from Aunt Amy when I was five. She would leave someone else in charge of her store for a few days so she could come and visit. She'd spend all her time with Joaquin and me because Momma was a waitress and usually had a boyfriend she wanted to marry.

One time when Aunt Amy arrived, Momma was at work, I was at school, and the boyfriend (Ryan) let her into the apartment. (He was the one with the video games.) Then Aunt Amy made the boyfriend disappear.

No kidding. Disappear.

She told me about it, but her account was very suspicious. We didn't see him for a couple of days, so I asked her, "Where did Ryan go?"

Aunt Amy laughed and said, "I went *boo*! And he disappeared." She tickled me and we rolled around on the sofa. Back then Joaquin didn't know very many words, so I couldn't ask him how Aunt Amy really did it.

"No really," I said, squirming out of her arms. "Where is Ryan?"

"Really, I said, 'Boo! Take your Wii and go!' And he did."

"When's he coming back?"

"Hope the stinker never does." And that made her remember. "By the way, Cheyenne, your room stinks. What's going on in there?"

She took me by the hand and walked me to my room. As soon as we got to the door, she started sniffing and choking to demonstrate. "Oh, this is so gross. How can you stand it?"

I didn't say anything, which is generally the best plan when an adult hasn't accused you of anything yet. If you start making excuses about the wrong thing, it makes more trouble for you.

"It's either a dead mouse or rotten food," she said.

I was still waiting.

"Don't just stand there looking vacant, Cheyenne. You're not in trouble. Just tell me where to look for the stinking dead thing."

Well, I knew exactly what it was. In fact, the smell had been troubling me for some time. But the tuna fish used to taste good, and I had learned that you couldn't ever be too careful about keeping food on hand in case Momma didn't think about eating for a few days.

I took Aunt Amy's hand and opened the closet door. She

gagged and held her nose when I lifted out the open can from my stash. She took it from me with two fingers and held it far out in front of her as she walked it into the bathroom, lifted up the toilet lid, shook out the rotten tuna fish, and flushed. Then she walked into my room and opened the window.

I was still sitting by my food hoard, counting how much stuff was left without the half-eaten can of tuna, when she sat down beside me on the floor. "What is all this, Cheyenne?"

"Food."

"Yes. I can see that. Why is it in this book bag in your closet?"

"I used to have it in my bottom drawer, but Momma hated all the ants that came trailing around. I had to move it where she wouldn't see the ants."

She lifted up two cartons of crackers that had ants dripping off the bottom. I thought that was a mistake and said so. "If you leave the cracker box in the bottom of the book bag and open it from the top, the ants don't always climb up there." Ants are easy to squash anyway. I don't hate them like I hate spiders.

Aunt Amy looked at me kind of funny, like she wasn't sure if it was the time to laugh or cry. She put her arms around me, then, and rocked me back and forth.

She must not like ants very much because she held the whole book bag out in front of her at arm's length as she carried it out to the back porch. Then she zapped everything that moved with a spray can of insect killer and threw away most of the food, which nearly broke my heart because it had been so hard for me to get a good supply. The rest of the cans she brought inside, washed them off, and put them back into the cupboard. I felt really discouraged and down. Now I'd have to start collecting food all over again.

She bent her knees until she was looking straight at me. That was the first time I noticed that she used the sight-dog approach too. She said, "Cheyenne, food that sits in the closet can get bacteria that will make you very sick. It can even kill you. Did you know that?"

Well, I didn't, of course. But I was listening, let me tell you.

"Promise me that whenever you open a can you'll either eat all of it or you'll put what you don't eat into the fridge."

"I promise," I said. It was a simple enough rule.

Then she got out a frying pan and said, "We're going to make pancakes. I'm going to write down everything I do, so you can make them when I'm gone." She let me drip the batter into the frying pan in any shape I wanted. We grated apple into some of the pancakes, and I liked that a lot. Joaquin woke up from his nap then and helped us eat up all the pancakes.

Later I heard Momma come home and I was glad Aunt Amy was there to tell her about Ryan. She cried and cried. So Joaquin and I cried in our beds too because the sound of your mother crying is just about the worst sound in the world.

Before she left, Aunt Amy taught me how to make scrambled eggs and toast. I was still pretty short and had to stand on a chair by the stove, but I wanted to learn how to cook more than just about anything in the world. After that she taught me how to cook a hamburger patty and how to put a potato in the microwave. I still keep the piece of paper she called a recipe in my book bag with my food hoard. Joaquin stuffed everything I handed him straight into his mouth. He was a good little Buddy.

## FIVE

# DEAD UNCLE DICK

The first time I ever heard about Dead Uncle Dick was when Aunt Amy had come for one of her visits and was telling Momma how to run her life so we boys would have "a more stable environment." Momma didn't like to hear that sort of thing and yelled back, "I'm doing the best I can. Can't you see that?"

Aunt Amy said, "Cheyenne is in first grade and still doesn't speak plainly. You need to have that looked into."

Momma turned around with her fiercest face and said, "Cheyenne is a very smart boy."

It feels very awkward to be right there when people are discussing you loudly, but I wasn't about to leave the room.

Aunt Amy said, "Of course he is, Coco. But you and I are used to how he speaks and can understand him. Have you asked his teacher if she can understand him?"

Well, I could have answered that question. But nobody asked me for the answer, which was "no." No, my teacher could not understand most of the things I told her. It was very frustrating. But too much was going on in front of me to even think about interrupting them with the facts.

Momma tends to throw things when she gets angry, and I could see she was about fifteen seconds away from slinging stuff. We were in the kitchen and I hoped it would only be the spoons. She'd thrown the forks at one boyfriend until he threatened to call the cops if she didn't stop.

I thought maybe Aunt Amy didn't know that about Momma because she kept right on going with her helpful comments. "Do you have any plans, Coco?"

"Plans? Yes, I've got plans!"

"Let's hear them."

"I'm getting married. That's my plan!"

I was alarmed about that. She was dating a stupid, greedy type right then, and I sure hoped he wasn't the candidate.

"You are?" Aunt Amy asked. "Who's the lucky guy?"

"I'll let you know when the time is right. It's just not right yet."

Aunt Amy put her arms around Momma and said really sweet-like, "Coco, honey, you're pretty and young, but you have to let that butterfly land on your shoulder. You can't go chasing it. I know you'll marry a wonderful man someday soon, but finding a man can't be your plan."

"Why not?"

"A plan is something like getting training so you can have a good-paying job."

"And just where would I get the money to do that?" I could see Momma was nearer to tears than to throwing spoons.

"Maybe you could get an advance on the rest of the estate." She meant when Grandma died. This idea alarmed me.

"No way am I going to ask Marc for any money. You know how tight he is. And he's the one who holds the purse strings."

I could see by Aunt Amy's face that she was getting way too eager about this idea. "Not completely," she said. "He may be the executor of the will because he's a lawyer, but Brett has a say-so in things."

Momma kind of sneered. "Brett always does what his big brother tells him to."

"And then there's Dick. He could—"

"Dick? He left my world when I was in kindergarten. He's been gone so long . . ."

Those words made goose bumps on my arms. "Left" and "gone" are two of the words people say when they mean "dead." I began listening even more carefully.

"He's your brother, your little boys' uncle . . ."

"Don't you think I haven't wished he were still here a million times?"

"I'm sure he would—"

"And when Grandpa died, Dick never even—"

"What do you know about things, Coco?"

"Shut your mouth, Amy. Just shut it. Dick is dead to me. Now shut your mouth about all of this."

There it was. Dead Uncle Dick.

"He might be coming back. I was talking to Brett not long ago and—"

"Back here?"

Was Momma worried or surprised? I couldn't quite tell, so I didn't know how to feel either. Later, when I explained to Joaquin about ghosts, he was very surprised and then very worried.

"This conversation is over." Momma didn't throw the spoons after all, but she walked down the hall and slammed her bedroom door hard.

"Tell me about Dead Uncle Dick," I said to Aunt Amy.

She was staring down the hall after Momma and said, "What?" real distracted-like.

"I want to know about Dead Uncle Dick," I said again.

"Sure, later, Cheyenne," Aunt Amy said as she followed after Momma down the hall.

Aunt Amy left the next morning without telling us anything more about Dead Uncle Dick, which was very disappointing. I have to say, it's been a real worry to know I have a dead uncle who might be coming back. He hasn't yet, but it's always in the back of my mind that one day he might show up. What would Joaquin and I do then? Run? Can a kid outrun a ghost?

You can't ask teachers about that sort of thing, and Aunt Amy didn't ever explain how ghosts come back. Joaquin and I don't even know if he's a good family ghost or a bad one. I do my best not to think about ghosts now that I'm older. But at night when I'm sorting through all the things that could happen to us, Dead Uncle Dick comes up as a regular worry.

# SIX

# JOKES

Momma didn't have a plan. I could see that plain enough. And if she didn't have a plan, I had to have one. The morning after Aunt Amy left, I counted my food hoard. Joaquin and I had had to use it regularly before Aunt Amy came. We didn't have much left, but hoarding food was the one plan I knew I could make work. Too bad I made a lot of mistakes.

I had found some ziplock sandwich bags in the kitchen drawer and told Joaquin that we were always supposed to keep one bag unzipped in each of our pockets in case we saw some food somewhere. One day I looked in the waste basket in the school room and found some perfectly good grapes and a partly-eaten hoagie sandwich. The trouble was that someone came in the room from recess right then and saw me taking food from the trash can. For the next two weeks the kids called me Trash Can Annie.

I would have carried that name forever if Momma hadn't

come home and announced we were moving. Right then. Right that very minute. That was one move I didn't cry about.

Joaquin and I grabbed our suitcases and put part of our food stash in each and then covered it all up with our clothes and stuffed animals. But with all the cans of food in them, the suitcases were too heavy for us to carry. Momma made us open our suitcases to find out why. When she saw all the food, she said, "Leave it. Take the groceries out. Just leave it! Come on! Hurry!"

So we went to another place to live and I had to start the food hoard all over again.

Every night as I was trying to go to sleep in the new apartment—and trying not to think about Dead Uncle Dick while I was doing it—I began to wonder if he might have some money he wasn't using. Aunt Amy had said that when Grandpa died, they divided up all the stuff into equal parts. So who got Dead Uncle Dick's pile? I don't think he walked in one day as they were dividing it up and hauled off his share. Unless that's a family story Aunt Amy hasn't told us about. But I don't think so. I think Dead Uncle Dick left his share of the money somewhere.

If you're a kid, there aren't many ways to get money. I've been working on this problem ever since Momma and I left Grandma and Grandpa's house. I understand that adults want to protect kids from greedy people who might want to work us hard and pay us little. But making it difficult for a kid to earn money isn't how to fix the problem. This is what I think: Kids should be able to make money if we want to, but other people shouldn't be able to ask us to work or expect us to earn money for them. It's a tricky problem, though, if you love somebody a lot, like Joaquin and I love Aunt Amy.

Even if I don't always do what grown-ups tell me to, I am very particular about listening to what they say. First reason: they have a lot of information. Second reason: they know how to get food and money.

Surviving your childhood depends on how quickly you can translate what an adult says into kid language. You can't take adult instructions directly. Here's what I mean. Suppose I have my sight-dog eyes trained on Mom's boyfriend who is treating her like sugar (the one with white canvas shoes and the gold watch). Aunt Amy comes to visit and yells at Mom that all the boyfriend wants is to get his hands on the new sports car my mother is buying. That's how adult information comes at you.

What to do next is the part most kids get wrong. I could do mean things to the boyfriend to make him go away. That's what you'd expect. Kid books have stupid stories like "Chapter Four: Getting Rid of Your Mother's Boyfriend." They even put that advice on TV, so kids are tricked into thinking it will work. The movies say that when a kid doesn't like his momma's stupid, greedy boyfriend, he should make a lot of trouble for him. The boyfriend will act foolish and your mom will see what his real qualities are and get rid of him.

That is a lie.

What actually happens is that when you make a lot of

trouble for the boyfriend, you get in a lot of trouble yourself. The truth is your mom has to decide to get rid of him.

But here's the important part. If he's going to be hanging around anyway, you might as well practice your money-making skills on him. I accidentally started working on my joke-telling technique when I didn't even know you could get paid for telling jokes in real life. I thought it was just a TV thing. This is where being a good sight dog comes in handy.

Okay, I've got my eyes trained on getting money so I can buy more food, right? Even though I think Momma's boyfriend is stupid and greedy, he's all I've got to work with, so I have to change how I think about him. I have to translate him into kid language. You do not tell yourself the lie that he's all of a sudden smart and generous. No. You think about what he wants most. You train your eyes to see what he is thinking about all the time. Be a sight dog on him.

Generally Momma's boyfriends think most about money and feeling good. If I tell him a joke that makes him laugh, he feels good and might dig in his pants pockets and throw me some change. Unless you're the kind of kid who likes doing mean things to a stupid, greedy boyfriend and then likes getting punished for them, don't treat him bad. Make him laugh. Once he gives you the first quarter, he'll give you more if you can make him laugh. That's what I taught Joaquin.

He might go ahead and steal from your momma anyway, but at least maybe he'll feel guilty about it because she was such a pretty thing and she had such a darn cute kid. The other way, he'll say she deserved it because she raised such a rotten kid.

Here's another warning: If you memorize an adult joke, it's pretty sure no grown-up is going to pay you. The problem with an adult joke is it makes you look like a trained monkey. So don't even bother with them.

Generic jokes, though, are completely different—that's a joke that fits everybody—and Joaquin and I have some that work no matter what.

You ask, "What is as big as an elephant but doesn't weigh anything?"

The boyfriend says, "I don't know."

If he tries to get smart and make a bunch of guesses, then you just keep watching him, keep on listening. When he gets done with his dumb answers that aren't even funny, you say the real answer: "An elephant's shadow." That's a generic joke because you can fit any animal into it.

Say your momma's new boyfriend has a Doberman Pinscher. If you put the name of the breed of his dog into the joke, almost for sure he's going to kind of chuckle. That's a good start.

Another kind of generic joke that Joaquin thinks is really funny goes like this:

Joaquin asks, "What is the difference between a dog and a microwave?"

The boyfriend says, "I don't know."

Joaquin says, "A lot." Then Joaquin fires at him all the pairs of opposites he can think of on the spot—like a spider and a jar of pickles, or a donut and an airplane, or a loaf of bread and a lawn mower. Just anything he thinks of as he's going along.

Sometimes that joke makes boyfriends irritated, so I don't ever use it. But Joaquin thinks it's hysterically funny. He's cracking up the whole time he does it, so sometimes he can get away with it. I told him he has to quit that joke after three times.

There's a rule: first time funny, second time silly, third time gets a swat. Sometimes he remembers; sometimes he gets the swat. But generally the boyfriend misses because Momma's watching.

Chicken jokes and knock-knock jokes are groaners, but sometimes they're good for warm-ups. Adults won't usually toss you any money for them, but it gets them smiling. Here is Joaquin's favorite chicken joke:

He asks, "Why did the dinosaur cross the road?"

The grown-up answers, "I don't know."

He says, "Because a chicken wasn't available."

Sometimes the grown-up will smile and say, "Hey, that's cute." Translated: "You're a cute kid, but the joke isn't funny," which is a limited way of looking at things.

This is my favorite knock-knock joke:

"Knock, knock."

"Who's there?"

"Cargo."

"Cargo who?"

"No. Car goes beep beep."

Laughing makes a person feel very good, which means that by now the boyfriend really wants your jokes to be funny so he can start feeling really good. Maybe it's because adults become kids again for a minute when they're laughing. I'm glad to know there's something both grown-ups and kids see the same way.

## SEVEN

# PET STORE

I'm different from other kids because I don't waste myself. When Aunt Amy gets better, I'm going to point out this quality. Some kids waste themselves by fighting with each other. I don't. Other kids aren't the problem.

I know you're thinking that I mean adults are the problem. That's only partly true. When it comes to grown-ups, some kids just love them all. Other kids hate them all on first sight. I don't think like that.

Grown-ups are more like guard dogs. They keep their stuff away from other people, so you can't just take what you need. And they follow their own set of rules, mostly—which can be confusing. Sometimes they want you to have stuff, like school teachers, and sometimes they don't.

The rule about fighting is that whether you win or lose, you always waste yourself. If I win, then I've got an enemy and all his friends to watch out for. If I lose, I've got everybody everywhere to watch out for. Besides, if I get busted up, I can't go to the doctor or the hospital. Momma didn't ever have insurance, and I'm not sure if Aunt Amy does. Anyway, it's better to be the safe kid—the one who gets what he wants.

I teach Joaquin how not to waste himself either. He's a pretty good learner. When I feel like punching him for saying something twerpy, I remember how it was to be a twerp and not know how to get the things I needed. Pretty crummy. Pretty hungry and lonely.

Things started to change after I'd been in school a while. I began to get an idea of how to learn about things, how to get information from the grown-ups. I discovered that knowing stuff is the main difference between a child and an adult—other than size.

About that time Momma had a new boyfriend who was kind of nice. Everything he did was really for him, but he knew enough to do nice things to other people along the way because that made it so much nicer for him.

He wanted time alone with Momma and that's what I wanted too. Instead of making it a competition, though, he bought Joaquin and me a whole lot of used movies and a DVD player for our little bedroom TV. That way we'd stay put for awhile, and he could be the big man in the house.

I knew I'd been bought, but while I was watching the movies I didn't care. Out of the whole stack of movies he gave us, I loved *The Lion King* best and Joaquin loved *The Hobbit* best. In fact, Joaquin and I got two of our best names from watching those movies.

Aunt Amy came for a short visit around then, and I

watched carefully to see if she'd say "Boo!" to this boyfriend and make him disappear too. I really hoped she would and that I could see how she did it. If it was a skill I could learn, I sure wanted to try it out. She didn't say it even once. Instead they sort of circled each other and snarled.

During the day Aunt Amy took us to the park or to museums or to special displays in stores. Like a huge store that had about a billion boats, every size a person could think of. At night she'd cook something delicious and then stay in the bedroom with us to watch the movies. We wanted her to see our favorites.

During *The Hobbit* she reached over and grabbed Joaquin's foot to tickle it and make him giggle. He kicked and squealed and wriggled, and I was starting to worry that the boyfriend would come stomping in. All of a sudden she took a look at what she was holding and said, "Joaquin, this is a hobbit foot! Stand up. I want to see this."

So Joaquin stood up on his two feet and Aunt Amy and I stared at them. It was true. Joaquin's feet were almost as long as his leg was up to his knee. She said, "Look at the feet on this puppy! If you grow into these feet, you're going to be a Great Dane!"

Hobbits are small people with big hairy feet who like to be comfortable and eat many times a day. After that, whenever Joaquin called himself HM, it no longer meant Hungry Man; it stood for Hobbit Man. When I grow out of a pair of shoes, he grows right into them. And he's four years younger than me. So, he's still HM.

The name I got from *The Lion King* has the initials LKC.

It's still a secret, so that's all I can tell you. Sorry.

The next morning Aunt Amy and Joaquin and I were sitting in the kitchen having breakfast when the boyfriend strolled down the hall. He tousled Joaquin's hair kind of casual-like and said, "So where'd you get this little fellow?" He said it in a way that anybody could tell he didn't expect an answer, but Aunt Amy gave him one.

"From the pet shop."

He stared at her hard. He knew she didn't like him and was being smart-alecky on purpose.

She said, "Yep, isn't that right, Cheyenne? We picked him up from the pet store a few years ago. Been with us ever since."

The boyfriend was dumb enough to look at me with a question on his face. Well, of course I'm going to agree with Aunt Amy. So there I was, nodding my head up and down for all I was worth. I blurted out the first thing I thought of: "His name is Buddy."

Ever since then, if Joaquin is annoying Aunt Amy, she'll look over at me and say, "Maybe we got him at the pound. What do you think?"

I always say, "No, I'm sure it was the pet shop."

Joaquin only cried about it the first time we teased him. Now he tries to punch us when we say it. He loves wrestling with Aunt Amy and so do I. Buddy is a private name. Only the three of us can use it.

## EIGHT

# FLOWER LADY

J ust before Christmas back when I was in third grade, my teacher said that she had someone she wanted me to meet. That does not always mean a good thing is going to happen. In this case, though, it was very good. She was a lady who works with kids like me to help them speak more clearly.

She had very light hair, so light it seemed transparent when the sunlight came through it. Her skin was bright pink, but she liked to wear grey clothes. I think if she'd worn bright, pretty colors, she could have gotten lost in a garden of flowers.

I really wanted to be able to tell jokes better so I could earn more money, so I listened carefully to everything she said. First we did some tests. They were very interesting. Nobody had ever asked me to do any of those things with my tongue before.

A few mornings later Momma came right into the school with me because she said she had an appointment with the speech lady. My Flower Lady had me repeat the tests from the day before while Momma sat behind me, watching over my head. They talked about me like I wasn't there, but this time I didn't feel uncomfortable because they weren't fighting. Besides, I was getting used to how grown-ups tend to do that.

Then the speech lady began asking me questions about what I liked to eat. She wanted to know all about our meal times and what we ate in our family. So I told her about Aunt Amy teaching me how to cook. And I told her about my food hoard and what was in it. And I even said that we don't sit at the table to eat unless Aunt Amy is there.

The speech lady said I could go to class then, and when I turned around to leave I caught a look at Momma's face. With her sitting behind me, I hadn't seen it before or I wouldn't have said any of those things.

Momma didn't usually come to walk me home from school, but she did that day. I saw her at the end of the hall, waiting. I was careful to only look down at her legs because I was afraid to look up any higher in case the look on her face was still the same. What really, really surprised me, though, is that she didn't say anything about what I had told the speech lady. She asked me if I'd like to go grocery shopping. I busted out with a "Yes!" that made the other kids turn and stare at us.

In the store Momma said she had gotten some really good tip money last night. Tips means the money she gets to keep for herself for being a good waitress. She had a whole pocket full of one and five dollar bills. It was the most money I'd ever seen in one spot before. She asked me what I wanted to buy. I told her that cans of food were too heavy to carry and too hard to open. I wanted food that was light and that Joaquin and I could open by ourselves.

At the end of the shopping trip I had wet food in shiny foil packages and dried food in plastic packages and Momma let me keep all of it in my bedroom. She even said we could eat our crackers in bed at night as long as we didn't attract ants. I asked her how to keep the ants away, and she said we had to vacuum more to get rid of crumbs. I knew how to run the vacuum from working at Aunt Amy's store, so that was the end of the ants. I don't miss them.

I saw the speech lady every day for the rest of the school year. Flower Lady's theory about why I couldn't speak plainly was because I had never learned to chew properly. My tongue didn't know what its job was, and I had to teach it. Our family was supposed to sit down at the table to eat real meals two or three times a day and I was supposed to chew everything I ate over and over again.

Right after that, our class had a lot of discussions on what my teacher called The Basic Food Groups. She had big colorful charts for each kind of food. We got to cut out food pictures from magazines and took turns arranging them around whichever of the big charts the food matched best. I found that very interesting and wished Joaquin was old enough to understand what I was learning.

But the very best thing that happened in school that year

was learning how to work the computers in the library. Most of my friends had computers at home and knew how to play games on them. But it was all new to me. My teacher said now that we knew about food groups, we were going to do research about food. Research is an organized way to get information about anything you want by looking in books or on the Internet.

The librarian sat beside me while I learned how to move the cursor and enter the words of the topic I wanted to find. I didn't think she would become suspicious if I asked to search for "How to Keep Food a Long Time." When she showed me how to look it up, the best words we found were "Food Storage."

You'd be amazed how much information there is about it. I wanted to know what foods store best. They have to stash away in a small space and they have to be light because you never know when you're going to have to pack them up quickly. Most important, they have to have lots of calories in them. If the food says "lite" on it, don't get it—even if it tastes good. It means they've taken out the food part of the food and you'll be hauling around stuff that leaves you hungry.

Momma didn't ever get into the habit of making meals very much, especially when a boyfriend was over. Those days Joaquin and I would sit on the closet floor with our food on a suitcase between us. We ate very slowly so I could chew and chew and chew. When there was no boyfriend, I'd cook something for Momma and Joaquin.

I think Momma's problem was that nobody had ever taught her how to do cooking. Grandma made wonderful food and so did Aunt Amy. But Momma had just never learned. I'll bet she'd have been really good at it by now.

## NINE

# ADVENTURES

I also learned about adventure stories that year. Let's put it this way: an adventure is what you call the scary stuff that happens to you. Grown-ups don't listen if you start to complain about your day; they do listen if you say you had an adventure.

My teacher was about to read the class an adventure story and was asking us what we knew about that kind of tale. We had gotten as far as talking about the main character being called a hero, and the class already knew that a hero is someone who is brave and smart and true. Then the teacher piped up that an adventure could sometimes be dangerous.

I shot my hand right up and said, "Being a kid is an adventure." When my teachers were still having a hard time understanding what I said, I had practiced not contributing very many answers. But sometimes sitting silent is harder than speaking. The Flower Lady said I was improving a lot, and that day I let my words come straight out this one time.

The teacher asked me very carefully, "Why does being a child seem like an adventure to you, Cheyenne?"

I said, "Because it's dangerous to be a kid."

"Can you tell me more about this idea?" she said.

"When you're a kid it's hard to get stuff. Almost everybody is bigger than you, so even if you do get stuff, somebody can take it away."

"What kind of stuff do you mean?" she asked.

I couldn't believe she was a grown-up and she didn't know the answer so without even thinking about it I said, "Food, of course. And money." That was way too close to telling two of our private wants. I wished I could have gulped the words back into my mouth.

"How does that happen?"

That was about the dumbest thing I'd ever heard an adult (who wasn't a boyfriend) say. No way was I going on with this conversation. I didn't answer. When she asked me again, I said, "What?" like I'd just walked in the room. That tends to discourage conversations with adults. They don't like having to repeat themselves. Even teachers, who are great repeaters of information, don't like to repeat everything leading up to the "what?"

That night Momma had a new boyfriend with her. I didn't like the looks of him. His nose was red and bulby, and he had a big belly hanging over his belt. Kind of gross. I don't know what Momma saw in him. But his pockets were sure full of change.

Joaquin and I were having a hard time keeping up our food stash because Momma didn't take us grocery shopping with her very often anymore and there wasn't much in the kitchen to cook. We really needed to earn some money, so that's why Joaquin and I didn't go right into the bedroom and start watching some old movie we had memorized completely by now.

We watched the boyfriend and Momma sit around smoking for awhile, and then Joaquin piped up in his little kid voice and said to the boyfriend, "Do you wanna hear a joke?"

Momma knew all our jokes, so she left. The boyfriend was lounging on the sofa with a drink in his hands and said, "So who's this little fart?"

Joaquin ignored the question. I had explained to him that some adult questions had no answers. Grown-ups use them as filler and don't expect answers anyway, so he should just go on like the boyfriend hadn't said anything. "Bet you twenty-five cents I can make you laugh."

The boyfriend said, "Bet you can't," even though I could tell he was hoping Joaquin could.

"Deal," Joaquin said and shook his hand.

We do that so the boyfriend will take us seriously. It makes it more like a business deal, which helps remind him to pay the twenty-five cents.

Joaquin turned toward me and I knew what he was thinking. The worm joke.

I looked up, all solemn-like, at the boyfriend and paused a few seconds. "Well, I've got one you won't have heard before." That's mostly true because it's one I thought up by myself. It works best, though, if Joaquin and I do it together.

I could tell the boyfriend was interested now, so in a nonchalant way I asked, "Did you know worms are both boys and girls?"

You don't want to make a boyfriend think too hard, so Joaquin took the attention off the boyfriend and piped up with, "What?" like I'd just said the dumbest thing in the world.

I was still being solemn. "Yeah, one worm can be both a boy and a girl at the same time."

Joaquin said, "Naw," real scornful-like.

"Yeah, it's true." I turned to the boyfriend like he already knew that. "Weird, huh?"

Joaquin swaggered his head a little, "Who says?"

I said, "Everybody knows that, don't they, Bob?" You need to say the boyfriend's name right then to make him get attached to the joke a little more.

Bob looked from me to Joaquin and back again, which is the signal to get going on the joke before he snorts and says, "Huh!"

So I jumped right in. "Well, one day all these worms were sitting in their desks at school. And the teacher says, 'All the girls sing.' So half of each worm stands up high and sings.

"Then the teacher says, 'Okay, now all the boys sing.' And the other half of the worm perks up and stands straight up, singing.

"The teacher gives everybody a turn: 'Girls.' 'Boys.' 'Girls.' 'Boys.'

"And then the teacher goes faster: 'Girls.' 'Boys.' 'Girls.'

'Boys.' All the worms start to flip-flop back and forth.

"And then she goes real fast: 'Girls.' 'Boys.' 'Girls.' 'Boys.' 'Girls.' 'Boys.' 'Girls.' 'Boys,' until the worms are flip-flopping just like crazy dancers!"

Joaquin and I think it's the funniest joke of all every time we tell it. Joaquin was cracking up, and I had a big smile on my face. I looked up at stupid Bob to see if he got it. The corners of his mouth were turned up, and he kind of huffed like it might turn into a laugh. I think his brain had figured out it was funny, but the drink in his hand was fuzzing up his brain too much to let his body know it.

He slumped back on the sofa and said in a bored voice, "Yeah, real funny." He took a big drink from his glass. He must have wanted us to make him laugh pretty bad because he kept the joke topic going. "So that's supposed to be funny?"

Joaquin is always honest—always. So he said, "Yes."

The boyfriend filled up his drink glass again and said, "Try me on another one. Make it funny this time, twerp!"

Joaquin went through all the jokes I'd taught him. The boyfriend kind of smiled at some of them and once or twice he said, "Hah!" like he might start into a laugh. But he didn't offer to pay. Not a single quarter. Not even a nickel.

Pretty soon Momma came into the living room and gave us "the sign," so I took Joaquin with me into our bedroom and we started watching one of the old movies for about the two-hundredth time.

Telling jokes for a living is a very tricky business. Sometimes there's a lot of money in it, and sometimes, for the same jokes, you don't get any money at all.

# TEN
# THIEVES

Later that night we heard the boyfriend and Momma making a lot of noise in the living room, laughing and dancing. In a while it got quiet so we opened the bedroom door a crack. Momma's bedroom door was open so we could see her lying on the bed with all her clothes on, sound asleep. We tiptoed down the hall to see if the boyfriend was still there. He was lying on his side, sprawled all over the living room sofa, dead drunk.

That's when I told Joaquin that it wasn't fair for him to hear all our best jokes and not give us a single penny.

Joaquin whispered, "I'll help him." Joaquin walked over to the man's pocket bulge where his wallet was and slid it out carefully.

Joaquin's hands are big for his age, but not as big as his feet, so he could slide the wallet out very smoothly. He opened it up and then looked at me. "How many jokes did I tell?"

"Twelve. That's all you know," I whispered back.

"How much is that worth?"

I was still learning the times tables but I made ticks with a pencil on a piece of paper and worked it out. "Three dollars," I said.

Joaquin opened the wallet and said, "He's got some ones." He handed me three one-dollar bills and took the piece of paper with the ticks on it. He turned it over and had me write on it: "You od 3 dollers. Thanks, HM."

He folded up the paper and put it into the wallet where the three dollars had been. Then he shoved the wallet gently into the boyfriend's pants pocket. We tiptoed down the hall and went to bed.

In the morning the boyfriend was already gone when we got up. It was Saturday and he had to work, but we didn't have to go to school. I had promised Joaquin I'd make him some pancakes if I could find the right stuff. We were both so hungry we could hardly concentrate on anything else except eating.

Momma was smoking at the table and looked up as we walked into the kitchen. She was very stern and held up the note Joaquin had left in the boyfriend's wallet. "Did you write this, Cheyenne?"

"Yes," I said.

"What does it mean?"

We explained how the boyfriend hadn't paid for any of the jokes and we were helping him be honest. Momma said we boys were the ones stealing money and should be punished. She didn't want any little thieves in the house. Joaquin is sensitive about that sort of thing and started to cry.

It made me mad to hear her talk to him that way. He's really little and he's the best one of us all at telling the truth. So, for the first time in my whole life I tried yelling at Momma like Aunt Amy does.

I remember it all clearly as being one of the worst things that ever happened to our family. Momma didn't back down. She defended the boyfriend the whole time. Joaquin said people should be honest and pay what they owed.

Momma said jokes were supposed to be free. I said we couldn't afford to give away the best thing we did that would earn money. Joaquin said that it had all been his idea to help the boyfriend be honest.

I said the boyfriend was a jerk and I hated him. Pretty soon the whole thing was so scrambled around that it turned inside out and upside down and none of it sounded reasonable.

It ended when Momma started coughing so hard I had to run to her bathroom to get her inhaler. She takes breathing medicine for asthma. She says smoking makes her lungs feel excited and also helps her breathe, but I doubt it.

# ELEVEN

# HEAVEN

The beginning of school that year was really good. My teacher was sweet and treated me like I was the LKC. I had thought about asking her to call me by those initials, but had decided to wait a month and see if her niceness held. The meaning of LKC was still a secret name then, which I wouldn't be able to tell her. You have to be very good friends with a grown-up for them to tolerate secrets. I don't know what it is about adults and secrets. Kids let each other have secrets, but adults just about go crazy. The last thing you want to do is let an adult know you have one.

As things turned out, none of that even mattered because Momma fell in love. She said this was the real thing and we were going to follow him to his home city. The first time I heard about it I cried myself to sleep because I was just getting used to my school. I'd already been through the name thing and now the kids didn't think about it so much. I was getting to like that school.

The next day when Momma told us the name of the boy-friend's city, it was the same one where Aunt Amy lived. I was so excited I ran around the living room a few times, and Joaquin jumped up and down on his big puppy feet. I wondered if Momma had forgotten she was no longer speaking to Aunt Amy or if she had changed her mind. Aunt Amy hadn't come to see us for quite a few months, and I was so excited for the move I could hardly sleep nights.

I'd lie in bed, listening to Joaquin sleep and imagining how it would be. First thing, Aunt Amy would cook for us. Then, she'd give me the complete information on Dead Uncle Dick. She'd let us come to her store after school so we wouldn't have to be at home alone, locked in the apartment while Momma was at work all evening. Right away she'd figure out ways for Joaquin and me to earn money. Maybe we'd get our food hoard so built up we could even spend some of the money we earned on a new movie. Things were going to be great!

And they were.

Momma's boyfriend had the apartment all ready for us. It was warm when we walked in the door. There was milk and juice and ice cream and everything else you could want, sitting there in the fridge. The cupboards were packed full of groceries. The phone and TV were already turned on. It was heaven.

Before I unpacked my suitcase, I looked up the name of Aunt Amy's store in the phone book. She didn't even recognize my voice. That's how much I'd changed! She sounded really happy and said she'd come for us as soon as she closed up the shop.

When Aunt Amy arrived, Momma introduced her to the new boyfriend and said they were just going out for dinner. Aunt Amy asked Momma right away if she could have Joaquin and me for the whole weekend.

Momma was happy and smiling that night and said, "Yes, of course, dear," and kissed Aunt Amy on the cheek. It was a huge relief to have their fight over with. I could tell Aunt Amy was surprised. Then Momma kissed Joaquin and me good-bye and smiled up at the man. He was a tall, handsome type, but he hadn't said much of anything yet.

Aunt Amy took us to her apartment and cooked the most delicious supper I've ever eaten. We sat on chairs at her table, which was covered with a white cloth, and used paper napkins on our mouths. She taught us the proper way to hold our forks and knives. We said "please" and "thank you" to each other all night. We ate real mashed potatoes and roast beef and fresh green beans—which, by the way, don't taste anything like the green beans out of a can. After chocolate cake, all three of us cleaned up the dishes and put the fresh food into the fridge in special plastic dishes with lids.

Aunt Amy took off the table cloth then, and we played Chinese checkers with colored marbles. The schools I went to had lots of board games and I was good at them, but Joaquin had never seen one before. He's a smart little Buddy and caught on quick.

All that food made us drowsy, so we couldn't play another game afterwards like we planned. Just before bedtime Aunt Amy gave us a cup of warm cocoa. She even had brand-new toothbrushes for us.

When I woke up on Saturday morning, I thought I was in heaven. Aunt Amy was cooking again—scrambled eggs and bacon with orange juice and all the toast and jam we wanted. She took us to a playground in the morning so we could run around and show off. Then we had a big lunch in a restaurant, and in the afternoon we went to a children's play. I didn't know that people would pay money to see kids up on stage, singing and dancing and saying jokes.

I looked over at Joaquin and he looked at me, and I could tell we were going to ask Aunt Amy how to get started in the business and how much they paid. Her answer was the only disappointing thing of the whole weekend. The children did it for the fun of it, she said. Maybe Momma had a point about how we should give away our jokes for free to her boyfriends.

Sunday morning Aunt Amy took us to a cathedral in the middle of the city. She said it wasn't really her church but she loved the music. All the men who were doing things up front wore beautiful white and gold costumes and spoke in a foreign language. I'd never heard a foreign language before, and Joaquin and I were fascinated by the sound of it. I listened as hard as I could, but it wasn't like pig Latin at recess that you can figure out right away.

When the choir sang, the sound whirled all around our heads and inside our bodies. The organ music made the floor vibrate and the marble pillars tremble. I started to cry. I couldn't help it. The joy inside me was full and spilled over. I didn't know there was anything that beautiful in the world. Aunt Amy handed me a tissue, and I bent over close to the floor and blew my nose in private.

When Sunday night came, my tummy was round and sticking out. Aunt Amy drove us home and helped us get our suitcases out but didn't come up with us. When we opened the door, Momma was sitting with the handsome man in the living room and lovely music was playing. The delicious smell of leftover supper was in the air, but I could tell from the table that the food was the already-cooked kind you bring home in paper cartons. Momma was wearing a beautiful dress, and I thought I could see the butterfly of true love sitting on her shoulder.

When I went to bed in the new bedroom with the fresh sheets, I relaxed into a feather pillow and fell asleep in two breaths. I finally knew what it was like to sleep through the night without waking up to listen for Momma coming home from work.

The next morning Joaquin and I went to a school nearby. I started to love it just walking down the hall, the first two minutes I was there. The teacher was very respectful when she introduced me to the other class members, and at recess nobody offered to punch me out because of my name. All the books she handed me were brand new. Even my pencils and eraser were new. Nobody's initials were dug in the desk and there was no gum under the seat. The floor was shiny and the chalkboards were white with dry erase markers in different colors. I tell you, it was heaven.

Aunt Amy paid us to work in her store. We got the same amount of money every week, without fail. I got more money than Joaquin because I had more skills, which Aunt Amy explained was fair. Joaquin was fine with it. He was just glad not to have to tell jokes for money anymore.

Aunt Amy took us grocery shopping, and we filled up our food hoard to the limit and stashed the book bags deep in our closet. After doing that, we felt completely comfortable. We didn't need to use any of our own food hoard because we could eat out of the cupboards and fridge. How could everything in our lives go from semi-miserable to absolutely great in so short a time? It was a mystery.

## TWELVE
# BUTTERFLY

The wonderful, happy time kept on and on, and Joaquin and I were almost ready to get used to it. The handsome man came for Momma on the weekends, and Joaquin and I spent every weekend with Aunt Amy. She always came to pick us up. We only saw this boyfriend from a distance. I touched his coat once, though. It was the softest coat I'd ever felt. I asked Aunt Amy about it, and she said it was called cashmere.

We felt safe all through Christmas holidays and even into the middle of winter. Valentine's Day we spent with Aunt Amy and she gave us a heart-shaped box of chocolates to share at home. When Momma came to the door to let us in, she was all alone. But she was wearing beautiful, long, sparkling earrings the boyfriend had bought her as a Valentine gift. He had to leave suddenly on a business trip, she said.

We never saw the handsome man again. Pretty soon the cupboards didn't have very much food in them, and I started to get worried. Momma never told us where the butterfly of true love had flown, but she looked sad and lonesome again most of the time. Momma took a waitress job at night, and things were sliding back to the old semi-miserable way again.

That is, all except for time with Aunt Amy.

Then she and Momma had another fight, and we weren't allowed to go over to Aunt Amy's any more. I thought I'd cry my eyes out. Momma wasn't happy about my behavior. She said I was getting too old to cry.

One day when Joaquin and I got home from school, none of the lights would turn on. The electricity was turned off, and I knew what that meant. We were going to move. Any day it would happen. I held onto myself tight so the big empty cold place in the bottom of my stomach wouldn't open up and swallow me.

The next day an even more terrible thing happened. Momma got sick. Not a little bit sick like a head cold where if you lie in bed and drink enough water, you figure you might not die. But a high-fever kind of sick where she was coughing all the time, night and day. She stopped going to work, and the only thing in the cupboards left for me to cook was pancake mix and water.

All that week Joaquin and I didn't go to school so we could help Momma get better. Finally I knew she was really going to die if I didn't think of something.

I went down to the street and found a taxi driver who would take all three of us to Aunt Amy's apartment. When we got there, I left Momma and Joaquin in the taxi because of course there was no money at all in Momma's purse to pay the driver.

When Aunt Amy opened the door, I threw my arms around her so long she had to peel them off. Then I told her Momma was sick and that Joaquin was staying with Momma down in the taxi until Aunt Amy came down to pay the driver.

When she opened the door of the taxi, Joaquin threw his arms around her too, and she had to look over his head to see Momma, who was coughing and coughing and coughing. Aunt Amy told me to get in the taxi, quick. She slid in the front seat and told the driver: "Take us to the Holy Cross Hospital. I don't think I'm exaggerating if I say this is a life-and-death matter. How fast can you get there?"

It was fast. I'd never ridden in a car going that speed before. It would have been a real adventure if Momma hadn't been slumped over on my shoulder, coughing her lungs out. As it was, I've never been so scared in all my life.

When we got to the hospital emergency entrance, Aunt Amy ran in and called for a gurney. That's a bed on wheels. They pushed it right out to the taxi and loaded Momma onto it. She couldn't stand up or make words.

# THIRTEEN

# BILLS

Aunt Amy helped us pack up all our things at the lovely apartment where Momma had been so happy. I said good-bye to my teacher at the good school. She handed me some of the work I had been doing so that I could transfer more easily to the school near Aunt Amy's place. This process interested me because before when we moved schools it was always so sudden that we didn't ever say good-bye or get papers or anything. We'd just appear at another school with no introduction, and of course they had to take us.

It took a few days before Momma started to get even a little bit better. She had to stay in the hospital for two weeks. Sometimes in the evening Joaquin and I were allowed to visit in her room. We found the new smells and sounds in the hospital very interesting. Aunt Amy would bring Momma's favorite lotion and carefully smooth it all over her skin. That made Momma smile, and I felt so happy because she wasn't going to die.

The doctor used words I didn't recognize, but Aunt Amy told me later that Momma had survived a special kind of pneumonia. It probably began because she was physically weak and emotionally distressed and her lungs were already damaged from asthma and smoking. Momma could go home with us, but she was supposed to have lots of rest, eat a regular balanced diet, and exercise every day.

The night after we picked up Momma from the hospital, I saw Aunt Amy making a bed for herself on the living room sofa. I felt sad that she was going to have to give up both of her bedrooms for us. Our family had pushed her out of her own place.

She looked at me sternly and said, "Stop it, Cheyenne. This is what family does for one another. You'd do the same if I needed help, wouldn't you?"

I said, "Yes."

And that is the truth. I have.

I liked my new school well enough. If you've been the new kid at half a dozen schools, you pretty well get everybody sorted out in the first half hour. If you don't, you've got big trouble ahead. After a week at that school, I could tell things would be okay.

One day after school Aunt Amy was sitting at the table with her laptop open and a stack of letters beside it. She hardly looked up when I came in.

"Whatcha doing, Aunt Amy?"

Her eyes stayed on the computer screen. "Bills."

"Where's Momma?" I asked Joaquin.

"In her room."

I knocked first and then opened the door to the bed-room. Momma was sitting in a chair by the window with a book in her lap. Sometimes when I look at Momma I think she is the most beautiful creature that ever lived. It almost takes my breath away.

Joaquin walked in first and put his arms around her and gave her a hug. "Hi, Momma," he said, stroking her hand. His were almost as big as hers.

Momma smiled at him and gave him a hug. I like watch-ing them together. When I'm in the middle of the hugging, it's hard for me to keep a balance on things. How I feel seems to tip and blur and get confused. But when I watch Momma and Joaquin together, it's like I know how to feel her kind of love.

I went over to her chair and looked out the window where she was looking. "Joaquin met me at the corner today. Did you see us coming up the sidewalk?" I asked.

"Yes, I did. You are very good to your little brother, Cheyenne. I think you're better to him than any of us."

She meant better than *her*. I thought about it a moment and decided it was one of those topics there's no use talking about.

I said, "I've got homework tonight."

Joaquin ran to our room for a book, and then I heard him close the door of Momma's room so he could have her all to himself.

I set out my homework books across the table from Aunt Amy and opened them to work. I looked up to check on her face just before I began and wished I hadn't. She looked so absolutely scared that my stomach dropped right down to a cold place in the bottom of my soul.

"Bills?" I asked.

"Oh, Cheyenne. You don't know the half of it."

"Maybe I can guess."

She looked at me sharply and said, "Why? What do you know?"

"Momma didn't have any insurance, did she?"

Aunt Amy sighed. "You guessed it. I don't know how you do it, Cheyenne. You're prescient."

That was a new word, but she said it like a compliment, so I didn't ask.

"The hospital bills and the doctor bills are going to go on and on for the rest of my natural life," Aunt Amy said.

"Why do you have to pay them?"

"When I took your mother to the emergency room and filled out all the paper work, I wrote my name as the person responsible. People should pay for what they get. Just not this much. This is paying too much."

"How much do you have to pay?"

"Even using the payment plans they gave me, spread out over the next eight years, it's going to take all my working capital."

"What's working capital?"

"That's the money it takes to buy the goods I put in my store."

"What about the rich uncles?"

"Who's got one of those?"

"Joaquin and I do. You know, Uncle Brett and Dead

Uncle Dick, and Uncle Marc." Aunt Amy just sat there with a blank face, so I said, "Stop teasing me. I mean the uncles. Your brothers, Aunt Amy."

She picked up a handful of bills. "I've already called them. Your uncle Brett is a beginning professor. He has a lot of little kids, including a boy about your age and a little girl about Joaquin's age. His wife is running for mayor in their town and that's taken every penny they can find. He says he has nothing in savings to help us."

"What about Uncle Marc? Isn't he rich?"

"Probably, since he's a big-city lawyer, but he says with low returns on his investments these days, all his working capital is tied up."

I couldn't right out ask her if Dead Uncle Dick might like to contribute, so I said, "We need another uncle. One with some spare money."

"Four is plenty," she said.

"Four?" This was a surprise. I could only think of three: Uncle Brett, Uncle Marc, and Dead Uncle Dick.

"Yes, four. Marc has a twin named Douglas who left home when I was little. But Dick's been gone now, let's see, he's been gone since . . ."

I was desperate for information on Dead Uncle Dick, as you can imagine, so I practically stopped breathing while I waited for her to tell about him. I waited, but she just sort of sighed, like she'd forgotten what she was going to say.

I prompted her, "So Dead Uncle Dick might have some money?"

"Who? Dick? Well, he's the oldest brother . . . probably

has a low cost of living over there . . ."

I wondered where that was. Maybe some kind of a ghost country. I always got the idea that ghosts never used money because they didn't have to eat and could float anywhere they wanted to. But Aunt Amy wasn't thinking about our conversation, really. Her thoughts were all on the bills. I tried to keep her focused on money, the way I was. "So maybe Dead Uncle Dick isn't using his estate money?"

"Dick has always worked literally on the other side of the world! I'd sure like to visit him."

I thought about how ghosts work on the other side of our world—one we can't see—and felt very alarmed that Aunt Amy would want to go there. Maybe if she had enough money on this side of the world, she wouldn't need to go find him there, so I said, "Is there any way we could talk to him when he comes to this side of the world? Ask him if we could use some of his estate money?"

"Who?" Aunt Amy looked up sharply. I was disappointed in how this conversation was going. She wasn't paying enough attention.

I said his name as plainly as I could: "Dead Uncle Dick."

Aunt Amy looked stern. "Why do you call him that?"

"Because you did." I said it very softly, so she wouldn't get mad. If I'd said it loudly she would have called it lippy talk. "I'd help you look for it," I offered. Maybe Dead Uncle Dick had hidden his share of the family estate in some safe place. I could imagine several possibilities. Maybe he had stuffed his money in a secret place in the family lake house, or under the boat dock, or in a hole under the roots of a tree.

Aunt Amy walked over to the cupboard and lifted out some pans to make supper. "What are you talking about, Cheyenne? Can you get some lettuce out of the crisper and tear it up for a salad?" I wondered why Aunt Amy didn't ever want to talk about Dead Uncle Dick. "What's Joaquin doing?" she asked.

"Reading Momma a story."

"He can't read yet."

"He memorizes the books I read to him. In a way that means he can read them."

"I don't know what Joaquin would have done without you."

"Stayed at the pet store and waited for another owner, I guess!"

That was one of our comfortable old jokes together. She laughed like I knew she would and said, "Maybe."

"So what about the estate money?" I asked, to get her back on track.

"It's all gone. You know that. One year of the high life in Las Vegas will do it."

I still have images and smells and sounds in my mind from that year. I said, "Maybe Momma could go home to the lake house and Grandma would take care of her."

"Yes, that's what I had hoped. When I called your uncle Brett to ask him about the idea, he said your grandmother isn't doing well. She appears to be fine physically, but her mind is starting to wander. It's called getting senile. That sometimes happens to old people, Cheyenne. She can't even take care of herself these days. Uncle Brett thinks Grandma and Coco together would be a disaster waiting to happen."

Dinner was ready and I went to call Joaquin and Momma. Joaquin is too big and heavy to sit on Momma's lap, so they were kind of snuggled together in the chair. I felt happy to see them like that. Joaquin was getting his chance to be a little boy. And Momma was getting her chance to be a good mother.

## FOURTEEN

# FLOWN

Momma was getting better every day. I knew it. I could tell. She was still very thin and her skin looked like it was made of glass, but she was definitely getting better. Joaquin and I were very careful of her, not to be noisy or jumpy. Aunt Amy treated her like she might break any minute.

Momma was tranquil. After seeing her with the handsome boyfriend, I couldn't say she was happy like when she had the butterfly of true love resting on her shoulder. But she was a kind of happy I enjoyed being around. A contented kind of happy. She was being taken care of and so were her boys.

Then spring began to come with flowers and birds and softer air. I could see that Momma was changing too. She was stronger, but restless. I told Aunt Amy about it, and we were sure it was happening because Momma was nearly well. That made us both feel relieved, like one big worry was nearly over.

At the end of April, Aunt Amy had to go out of town for a buying trip for the store. "What do you think, Cheyenne?" she asked. "Will you and Joaquin be okay without me for five days?"

I said we would.

"You're going to have to make your own breakfast and pack yourself a lunch and get yourself off to school. Then you're going to have to cook supper and see about baths and bedtime. I'll have casseroles in the freezer that you just put into the oven and heat. But you've got to make sure you all sit down and eat healthy food."

"I can do it, Aunt Amy."

Just then we looked up and saw Momma standing there listening.

Momma said, "Have you forgotten that I'm the adult here, Amy?" She said it in a dreamy sort of way. She could have yelled or been sarcastic, but the place where the idea came from must have been limp or maybe hollow.

Aunt Amy put her arms around Momma and said, "I'm sorry, Coco. That was insensitive of me. Please don't be mad."

Momma looked at me through Aunt Amy's arms and smiled. "Cheyenne has always been my little man, and now he's getting so tall." Joaquin threw his arms around Momma's legs, and she looked down. "Here's another strong little man."

After I had tucked Joaquin and Momma in their beds, I watched Aunt Amy pack her suitcase. I got to stay up half an hour later than Joaquin did because I'm older. He was okay with it when I explained it to him. Aunt Amy was folding a pretty blue sweater. I told her not to worry about us. We'd be just fine as long as there weren't any boyfriends in the picture.

Aunt Amy laughed. Then she turned serious. "If there's any trouble at all, call me. I'll call you every night before you go to bed. In an emergency you know how to dial 9-1-1, right? I'm putting some emergency money in this drawer," she said. She slipped some twenty-dollar bills in the side table. I'd count them later.

The morning was sunny when Aunt Amy left. Joaquin sat at the kitchen table, eating our cereal before school. And Momma was out of bed, dressed, and had brushed her hair into long black silky curls. It made me happy to see her like that.

Aunt Amy called every night like she promised and always asked to talk to Momma, not me. I think Aunt Amy was trying to make it up to Momma for having been insensitive about the household instructions she had given me. Maybe Aunt Amy thought she was helping Momma prove she was the adult.

The morning Aunt Amy was due to come home, Momma was smiling in the kitchen when Joaquin and I went in to make our breakfast. We didn't have to make it, though, because she had cereal boxes and juice set out for us on the table. Everything was so nice. I looked at how dressed up she was and asked her if she was going out to look for a job or something. She smiled and said, "Yes," and then she looked like she was going to cry. I didn't want her to do that, so we kissed her and hugged her good-bye and left for school while we were all so happy.

Momma hadn't come back from job hunting when we came home from school, so I spread peanut butter on one piece of bread while Joaquin spread jelly on the other. We smacked them together and cut them into really interesting shapes. Then I started on my homework, and he sat in the big chair and read his memorized books aloud. I kind of listened and kind of didn't.

Momma still hadn't come home, and it was nearly dark, so I turned on the oven, placed the last casserole inside it, and set the timer. There was something about that empty dark cold space in the freezer that made a little part inside me wake up worrying.

Aunt Amy called to tell us that one plane had been late, which made her miss the one she was supposed to get on next, so she'd be home in the middle of the night. Joaquin and I were just fine with that and went to bed. We expected she and Momma would both get home in the middle of the night. We would hear them talking and we'd roll over to finish sleeping. Then in the morning, we'd wake up to all kinds of good Aunt Amy smells coming from the kitchen.

When I woke up everything was totally silent, so I went to look for Aunt Amy and Momma. I found Aunt Amy sitting in the big chair, dressed, and wide awake, like she hadn't ever gone to bed. She looked at me and didn't smile, and that started the big cold freezer place in my belly opening up.

Then she put out her arms to me and I went to stand by

the side of the chair where she could put one arm around me in the sideways hug I like best.

"Where's Momma?"

"I don't know, Cheyenne. Is Joaquin awake?"

"Not yet."

"You'd better get him up."

Joaquin was out of bed, sitting in the bottom of the closet, looking at our food hoard. He hadn't started counting cans, yet, but I could tell he planned to. I took him in to Aunt Amy.

"Where's Momma?" he asked her, right off.

"I don't know. And that's what I need to talk to you boys about."

Aunt Amy's voice had a big scratch in it like she was holding it tight. I looked at her face, and it was twisted up in the way people do when they won't let tears leak out natural-like.

Joaquin reached up and patted her face. "Don't cry, Aunt Amy. Did you have a bad time while you were away?"

"No," she said, "my buying trip was good. But I had a couple of letters waiting for me when I got back that I've got to talk to you about." She picked up some folded pieces of paper, the kind with blue lines that you pull out of a spiral notebook. "When did you see your Momma last?"

We told her about breakfast and how nice and dressed-up Momma looked when we left for school. When she wasn't home when school was over, we did our homework, ate the last casserole, and put ourselves to bed. I said that Momma probably got work right on the spot because she was an excellent waitress and very pretty and would be coming home to sleep while we were having breakfast.

Aunt Amy said she hoped Momma had found work that fast, but that she wasn't going to be coming home for a while.

Joaquin said, "When?"

"These are letters from your Momma." Aunt Amy opened one and read, "Dear Cheyenne and Joaquin, I want you boys to always remember how much I love you. I am sorry I haven't been a good mother to you. Aunt Amy will be a way better mother to help you grow up. But remember me. Remember that I really do love you and it nearly kills me to say good-bye. I think you will have a better life with Aunt Amy. All my love, Momma."

The dark, cold space inside me opened up so wide, I thought I was going to fall into it forever.

Joaquin didn't get it. He kept pestering Aunt Amy with where Momma had gone and when she'd be back. Finally Aunt Amy started to cry. Whenever Joaquin asked her anything, she'd say the same thing over and over again. "I don't know where she's gone. Her letter to me says she's a no-good mother and she doesn't want us to look for her. Ever. That's all she said. Honest."

I went over to the window and looked out into the trees, like if I looked hard enough she wouldn't have flown. I tried to see her through the branches coming up the sidewalk, all tired out from her all-night waitressing job. I tried to hear her coming in the door, the swishing of sheets as she crawled into bed, too tired to say a word.

I didn't hear anything except Aunt Amy's sobs and

Joaquin pestering, and then I started to cry too.

But crying isn't safe if the grown-up in charge of you is also crying. I took a good look at Aunt Amy to see if she had any plan inside of her. She said that if she hadn't gone on the buying trip, everything would have been different. And then Joaquin said if he hadn't been born things would have been different. So then Aunt Amy sat up quick and dried off her face.

I could see from what Joaquin had said that any little thing you do can maybe make all the difference and can maybe make no difference. You never know. You just have to keep on going.

## FIFTEEN
# WALKER MEN

Aunt Amy called a lot of people. Sometimes she'd cry
and sometimes she'd be calm and sometimes she'd be
pretty angry. It was Saturday, so Joaquin and I didn't have
to go to school. He sat in the bottom of the closet with the
light on and made big towers with the cans and packages in
our food hoard. Even though he kept the door shut, I could
tell what he was doing because I could hear the cans tumble
down when the tower got too high.

I turned the high back of the big chair around so Aunt
Amy couldn't see me sitting there, listening to all her phone
calls. After awhile I got hungry and set the table for breakfast. I started cooking pancakes and pretty soon the smell
got down the hall to Joaquin. He walked into the kitchen
and sat down at his place and said, "Okay, when's Momma
coming back?"

Aunt Amy and I just looked at him.

"I'm too hungry to wait for her. Let's eat." He was chatting away and eating, so we all started in on our stacks of pancakes and syrup. I asked Aunt Amy as casual-like as I could who she was talking to. She said, "Mostly my big brothers."

"Did you tell them your plan?" I was hoping she had one.

"We worked one out while we talked. Your mother gave me legal custody of you boys. Your uncle Marc is going to get all the papers ready for me to sign."

Just then the phone rang and while she was talking, Aunt Amy's face started to look bright and happy all of a sudden. When she hung up and came back to the table, she said, "That was Aunt Sandy. She's organizing a get-together of the Walker clan at the lake house for the Easter holidays and asked me if we could make it."

"Can we?"

"You bet. There's going to be more cousins there than you can imagine!"

And that was the truth of it.

I will always remember the drive from Aunt Amy's apartment to the lake house because we all felt empty and sad and somehow free at the same time. Momma wasn't with us, but in a way she never had been. It would have been strange to have had Momma along. But I missed her like a part of my own body was gone. I know that sounds like opposite things, but this was one time when two opposite things were true.

Someday I would like to take a long drive where I could wander around and see anything I liked along the way. But Aunt Amy didn't have extra money, she said, so we could only spend for things we had to have, like tanks of gas and grocery store food, and a medium-cheap motel for one night on the way.

The lake was still and smooth when we drove into the little community where Momma and Aunt Amy and their big brothers had grown up. The cousins and aunts and uncles treated the three of us like we were strange and precious. I felt more on the spot than I had expected, like people were watching me a lot to see what kind of person I was.

After awhile I caught on to what our job was. I told Joaquin that we had to show people that we came from a very nice family too. I told him we could do a good job if we were careful not to waste ourselves. He looked at me with question mark eyes, so I said that if we acted loud and stupid and talked too much, we would waste ourselves. We needed to listen to what people said so we could understand how things were. The first day we stood together all the time to help each other with this job. But then things got noisy and fun and we were all running around like we'd been cousins our whole lives.

Brady, the cousin my age, was the most fun of all. We sat together at the table and slept in the same single bed at night. He showed me right away which trees were the best climbers, which closets had big cracks for spying on people, and the drawers where Grandma kept the sweets. Best of all, he thought I had good ideas.

One morning his mom called him to take care of his little twin brothers, Biscuits and Gravy. I was about ready for some time by myself, so I sat on the bottom step of the big staircase, thinking about how I'd been a baby in that house.

Some of it was familiar, yet the sizes were all changed. And of course Grandpa wasn't there to sing "The Boy Named Sue" for me.

I was thinking about all of this when I felt footsteps shaking the boards a little. I decided not to look up, but the adult sat down beside me. It was Uncle Brett, Brady's dad. He didn't say anything, so neither did I. Soon it got hard to do any thinking with him there and I was almost ready to say, "Okay, good-bye," when he took a breath and said, "So do you remember being little in this house?"

I jumped. It was like he had read my thoughts. "I remember Grandpa singing 'A Boy Named Sue' to Momma."

Uncle Brett laughed and said he remembered that too.

"Did she really hit him?" I asked.

"Probably, knowing your momma. Is that how you remember it?"

"Yes, and Grandpa just laughed."

"I miss him when I come to the lake house."

He meant that he missed his dad. Uncle Brett's eyes smiled all the time, so I said, "I wonder what he'd say about Momma."

"He'd tell her to come home."

"Do you think she will?"

"You might be quite a bit older when she does, Cheyenne, but I think she will come home."

"I wonder what Grandpa would say about me."

Uncle Brett looked at me for a minute. "He'd say Cheyenne was a classic Walker man, smart and handsome."

I turned to give Uncle Brett a look-over then to see what

kind of an uncle he was. What he said was a compliment for Grandpa and himself, but he really meant it for me. He was choosing me as a nephew. I felt happy, like I wanted to stay in that house the rest of my life and grow up to be a Walker man.

After a while I sang the first part of "A Boy Named Sue" for Uncle Brett and then asked him whether Grandpa had a special song for Momma.

Uncle Brett thought for a while and then brightened up. "There's a bluebird on my shoulder . . ." he sang.

All of a sudden I could hear Grandpa singing to Momma as she'd come down the stairs for breakfast. I could see Momma's face again, how she'd purse her lips tight and clap her hands over her ears, as though she couldn't hear him that way. I hadn't cried about Momma since the day when Aunt Amy first read her letter to us. But when Uncle Brett sang that song to me, his arm around my shoulders, I put my head down on my knees and cried.

## SIXTEEN

# SPYING

The next morning all the aunts and uncles went into the living room and shut the door. They were going to have a family meeting and nobody was supposed to make loud noises or knock on the door. Brady and the other cousins went outside into the morning sunshine, but I needed to listen.

They hadn't given us much notice that it was going to happen, so figuring out where Joaquin and I would be able to hear and see the best was a tricky problem. If kids move at a regular slow speed, though, adults tend not to notice them. And that's how we got up these nearly vertical stairs into the loft without anyone telling us to run outside and play. We were seen, probably, but not really seen.

The loft was a narrow room that ran around two sides of the great big living room. It had a railing around the edge of it so nobody would fall off into the room below. There were lots of single beds running end to end right next to the wall, all the way around the loft. Every once in a while, there was a little square table with four chairs so people could play games or read or draw or eat snacks. I really liked being there and wished they'd given it to Joaquin and me for our bedroom. Of course, it wasn't completely handy because there weren't any closets. And at night it wouldn't be all that cozy because there would be too much space around me.

Joaquin and I quietly slipped underneath a bed right next to the ladder-stairs. If we raised our heads a little, we could see the tops of heads and some faces between the railing posts.

Uncle Marc started to speak. He said that as the senior member of the family (I told Joaquin that meant he was the oldest uncle), he would open the meeting. He thanked Aunt Amy on behalf of the family for her help with Coco over the years and her wonderful relationship with the boys. He said that Amy's role in keeping the family together showed tenacity. If it weren't for her, the family would have completely lost track of Coco and the boys. Joaquin and I bumped shoulders and smiled under the bed. That meant the family was glad we got found.

Then Uncle Marc asked for an accounting of her expenses. Apparently Aunt Amy expected this, because I heard paper rustling and pretty soon everybody had a copy. People were silent and read for a while.

Grandma Walker couldn't stay quiet, though. She said, "Coco's snowball bush is blooming. Did you see that, Marc?"

He nodded but didn't look up.

"Did you see it, Brett?"

He looked up sort of confused because he hadn't been listening.

"We'll have lots of pansies around the boat dock this year. And the mallards are green again."

Joaquin looked at me with a question in his eyes.

"Mallards are ducks," I explained.

"Do they change colors?"

"I don't think so."

"I thought pansies were flowers."

"They are. She changed subjects."

"Where's William?" she said, looking around the room. "Is he out on the boat this morning?"

Everybody had stopped reading Aunt Amy's papers, but nobody said anything, so Grandma went on: "Brett, were you out fishing with your father this morning?"

Uncle Brett answered her extra softly, "No, I wasn't, Mother."

"Tell William we'll be having lunch late today. He never did like a late lunch. Did you ever know the man to like a late lunch, Sandy?"

"Who's Sandy?" Joaquin asked.

"Shhhhh! Uncle Brett's wife."

"The chubby one holding the great big baby?"

"That's her."

"She looks cheerful."

"Yeah," I said. "Now don't talk."

Aunt Lana—the skinny aunt—turned to her husband, Uncle Marc, and asked in a starchy kind of voice, "Marc, perhaps William Junior could spend some time with his grandmother this morning?"

Cousin Bill was the oldest cousin, sixteen, and named after Grandpa. He didn't talk to the younger cousins much when we ran by, so we kind of treated him like a tree or a duck or something.

Uncle Marc stood up and said, "Good idea, dear. I'll call him."

Pretty soon Cousin Bill came into the living room and whispered something into Grandma's ear. She looked all around the room and smiled happily. "Now that everyone's playing nicely I'll go slice some carrot sticks for William's lunch."

Cousin Bill looked quickly at his mother who whispered, "No knives." He nodded. With his arm gently around his grandmother's shoulders, they walked out of the family meeting.

Uncle Marc said, "Are we through reading over the expenses list?"

Everyone nodded. They talked on and on about how to repay Aunt Amy for Momma's hospital bills. Finally they agreed to a plan, but it would take about a year.

"Are you okay with that, Amy?" Uncle Brett asked.

"Not really. I'm totally strapped for cash," she answered. "In my business, if you don't have new stock every week, you lose customers. Is there any other way you can loosen up some money?"

"Not at the present," Uncle Marc said, "but next quarter earnings might change things somewhat. I know a banker in your town. I'll be in touch with you on that." And that was final. Nobody said anything else about money.

Aunt Sandy stood up and gave Aunt Amy a hug, the large baby squashed between them. She said, "The boys seem to be doing really well, Amy. You've got such a way with them."

Aunt Lana walked by and shook Aunt Amy's hand. "We're all extremely grateful for everything you've done."

Uncle Marc grabbed her around the shoulders in a one-arm hug. "Hey there, little sister," he said. "Take care."

When it was Uncle Brett's turn, he held her in a big bear hug. "Amy, we love you. You know that, right? If you ever want to talk, or, well, anything . . . don't hesitate to call." Then he said, "If the rest of the family were here, especially Dick, I know they'd be proud of you too."

There it was. Dead Uncle Dick might be interested in what was going on in the family.

Aunt Amy snuffled a response. "I love you guys too," she said.

I poked Joaquin. "Did you hear that?"

"Yeah," he whispered.

"Maybe they like Dead Uncle Dick."

"Are you scared of him?"

You have to be honest with Joaquin, so I said, "Well, not as much, anyway. Are you?"

"Same."

We waited until the room had cleared before we crawled out from under the beds. We had dust bunnies all over us. But we ran outside in the sunshine until they all fell off, so who cares.

Brady and I explored the whole lake shore before the vacation was over. We even made a map of where important spots were. I didn't tell him I needed the map to find Dead Uncle Dick's estate treasure, but he really liked the idea of the map. We marked out the shape of the lake and houses, and then we started in on the important stuff like suspicious trees and rocks. We found a sort of cave that had soda cans nobody had drunk yet. Brady and I figured they were left over from a party and people had forgotten them, so that meant they were ours. We made the little cave our snack station.

If I could have lived forever at the lake house with Brady, my life would have been a super duper good one. But pretty soon we got in Aunt Amy's car and drove back to the city, where we went back to school and lived in an apartment that didn't have Momma in it anymore.

# SEVENTEEN
# BLISS

Just before school was out for the summer, Aunt Sandy called and invited us to spend the summer at the lake house with their family. She had just won the election for mayor of their town, but she wanted the children to have an old-fashioned family holiday just like every summer.

Aunt Sandy said that she and Uncle Brett were planning a split schedule so that each would have working time in town and playing time with the children at the lake. Both parents would be at the lake house on the weekends.

When I heard Aunt Amy say it might be too much work for Aunt Sandy to have Joaquin and me stay all summer, I fell on the sofa and clutched my stomach. Joaquin started to dance around her chair, begging, "Please, please, please."

I said, "Day camp for three months is going to be very expensive," which helped her thinking. Then she called Aunt Sandy back and said we boys wanted to come but that she was still worried about imposing.

Aunt Sandy said that when you already had five children running around, two more wouldn't make that much difference. Aunt Amy still didn't get it. She said she thought we'd be too much extra work. I held my breath.

But Aunt Sandy spelled it out in dresses. If you usually had an inventory of two hundred fifty dresses, a hundred more would make the selection richer and more interesting. Aunt Amy understood that. When she hung up the phone Joaquin and I were so happy we jumped around and flopped on the sofa over and over again.

When Aunt Amy put us on the bus, she said, "Cheyenne, I know you can handle this just fine. You've been tending your little brother all his life. Just don't talk to anybody except the bus driver, and don't let Joaquin out of your sight." We both kissed and hugged her good-bye.

When we sat down in our seats, I looked over at Joaquin and mouthed the word "Sorry." He knew exactly what I meant. Even Aunt Amy didn't quite understand what our relationship really is. I never "handle" or "tend" him. He's always been like me—only in a smaller body. He understands everything I tell him. A great little Buddy.

We went to sleep on the bus when it got dark. It had a tiny bathroom at the back and everything. The next morning after we ate the breakfast Aunt Amy had packed, we brushed our teeth and watched out the window. We could tell when the little town was coming up because we'd been on this road only a few months ago, on the way to the family reunion with Aunt Amy, and we recognized the shape of the hills.

Aunt Sandy picked us up at the bus stop, and Brady was

in the car with the other cousins. Even though he was a year older than me, he was turning out to be the best cousin you could ask for. We had only seen each other once before at Easter time, but it felt as if we'd been living next door our whole lives.

We did everything together that summer, from sleeping out in the tent all night to getting poison oak on our private parts when we peed in the bushes instead of coming into the house like we were told to.

We didn't eat at regular times like with Aunt Amy, and we didn't eat at hardly-ever times like with Momma. With Aunt Sandy we ate all the time. It was the same when it was Uncle Brett's week to stay at the lake. They set out food for us all day long. No matter what time of day we ran into the kitchen, there was always something set out to eat.

Sometimes it was cookies and milk. Sometimes it was ants on a log. At first I wouldn't eat those—my experience with ants in my food hoard being what it was—but then I found out it was just celery filled with peanut butter and a few raisins stuck along the top to look like ants. Other times it was apple slices with soft cheese or little baby muffins that you could eat in two bites. There was food everywhere, any time of day—which was a good thing because Aunt Amy wouldn't let Joaquin and me take the book bags holding our food hoard with us on vacation. She must have known we wouldn't need them.

When it was a sit-down meal time, Aunt Sandy or Uncle Brett would blow on an old conch shell Grandma and Grandpa had brought back from their honeymoon in

Hawaii. We'd hear the long mellow honk filtering through the lake trees, and that was our signal to run as fast as our lungs would let us to the big kitchen. We had to stand behind a chair and wait for everybody else to get there, somebody said a prayer, and then we fell into our chairs and ate up everything in sight.

The twins were the hot spot that summer. They had real names, I'm sure of it, but their family called them things like Ham & Cheese, Stars & Stripes, Bread & Butter. Anything that you usually said together is what they got called.

The morning they dumped out all the pans in every bottom cupboard in the kitchen and then ripped open five packages of dried Jell-O to pour into them, Uncle Brett called them Gin & Tonic. He said he needed some. He also said they were his Shock & Awe packages. Brady translated for me: the family hadn't expected to have any more babies, when all of a sudden, two years ago, along came Tuck & Roll.

Privately, Brady and I called them Burp & Fart. But we didn't say it in front of Aunt Sandy. She claimed they would grow up to be people we would be glad to have for friends, but Brady and I doubted it completely.

Joaquin had a girl cousin his age—Carmen—and at first I thought she was going to dump him with Brady and me. But after a while she could see what a good little Buddy he was, and they ran around together everywhere. They particularly liked making cookies. Aunt Sandy is a very good-natured person and helped them make cookies every single morning until they got tired of doing it.

Then for a few weeks Joaquin and Carmen were sent to

the garden to pick the peas. They thought that was the best fun in the world. Most of the peas got eaten or went whipping through the air like bullets, but Uncle Brett didn't say boo about the seventeen peas they'd bring back in the bottom of the bucket.

Brady and I showed Joaquin and Carmen the tadpole pools we discovered near the shore of the lake in the flat parts around the rocks. We watched them grow from tails-on fishes to tails-off frogs. We brought back a lot of them to show Adele, Brady's big sister, who was almost twelve. This was particularly interesting for us after we discovered how much she didn't like to touch, look at, or hear about tadpoles. From then on she was the total focus of our tadpole progress report.

Adele spent a lot of her time keeping track of Grandma, who sort of puttered around in her own world and made strange comments. Grandma was sweet to everybody, even if she never knew which name to call any of us. She was totally mixed up all the time.

Every weekend when both Uncle Brett and Aunt Sandy were at the lake was the best time of all because he would give us swimming lessons a couple of times a day and she would take us out in the canoes. The rule was we could splash on the edges of the lake during the week, but we had to wait for both parents to be there, with one watching us, before we could swim or boat. I'm good with rules that make sense, and I told Brady I would be fine with that one. I told Uncle Brett and Aunt Sandy we'd be sure Joaquin and Carmen kept the rules too.

After the swimming lesson ended, we liked to float on our backs with the sunshine baking us. Then we'd roll over and get our faces and chest cold so that we could roll back and start the toasting all over again. I'd never been around that much water before. It was an amazing thing to feel the weight of a whole lake being whipped around during a summer storm and then the next day to lie flat on top of it again, the weight completely underneath me.

At Easter time when I'd first had Brady make the big map with me, we told the adults it was a treasure map because they needed some kind of a reason for what we were doing. This summer I considered the possibility they might help us if they knew all the facts. Well, some of the facts, maybe. And then I came to my senses!

Considering the way Momma and Aunt Amy had not responded to the topic of Dead Uncle Dick, there wasn't any use bringing up the subject with two or three more relatives. Aunt Sandy and Uncle Brett might have limits I didn't know about.

I decided to be careful about talking too much about Dead Uncle Dick, even to Brady. I just said the lake house looked like a place where somebody might leave a treasure and that we ought to hunt for it. Brady had a good imagination and didn't question me at first about why I thought there might be a treasure there. After a month of this, one morning Brady told me the treasure hunt was stupid and he was quitting the project.

I had no choice. I had to tell him about Dead Uncle Dick and his part of the estate money. Brady was very enthusiastic after that. He said Dead Uncle Dick used to be alive, like at Grandpa's funeral, but that had been a long time ago and nobody had seen him since. We checked it out with his dad, who said it was true.

Brady and I combed every nook and cranny of that property for the estate treasure. Within a few weeks we knew the contents of every closet, every shelf, every drawer, every under-bed. When no treasure materialized, we hunted the grounds clear down to the boat dock.

By the end of the summer, Brady still didn't seem disappointed not to find anything, but I was. I needed to find that money more than he would ever know. Aunt Amy needed it, and no one was ever very specific about what to expect from Dead Uncle Dick.

Joaquin and I felt like part of the family package, like we were as naturally there as the mosquitoes and the tadpoles —which were funner. I felt like I was somebody else, like it must not really be me having this much fun.

## EIGHTEEN
# FRENCH ARRIVES

I knew the summer was nearly over because the leaves had changed sound when the wind blew through them. A little dryer and crisper. But I refused to let myself think about any plan that was bigger than what Brady and I would do that very day.

One Saturday morning at breakfast, Uncle Brett and Aunt Sandy told us we were to stay after breakfast for a family council. I had never been invited to one, but the one I'd spied on last Easter had been very interesting. Brady kind of groaned, but he sat back down beside me and we both waited.

Uncle Brett smiled around the table at us, but that wasn't new—he couldn't help himself from smiling when he looked at all of us children. Then he said that there was going to be a change in the family that even his kids didn't know about. That got their attention.

It sure got mine. Was one of Brady's parents going to

disappear or something? They'd be lucky to get a warning. Momma hadn't even given Joaquin and me a hint. I looked over at Joaquin sitting beside Carmen, and I know he was just about ready to cry for how sad Carmen was going to feel. He might even cry for himself too because we'd been having so much fun with two parents around, even if they weren't really ours.

I was too busy thinking about Dead Uncle Dick to consider crying. What if the change Uncle Brett was talking about would be Dead Uncle Dick appearing or something? That could be it, so I held myself absolutely still.

Uncle Brett leaned forward like he hoped his children were listening carefully. Everybody was, except for Thunder & Lightning, who squirmed all the time. He said that with the extra money from Aunt Sandy's job as mayor, they could pay the new car off and would have just enough money to hire a nanny. She would be an extra driver in the family and a tutor.

Nobody said anything. They didn't look sad or happy. Just puzzled. I was puzzled too because that sounded like three people were moving in, which would make their house very crowded.

"Not just any old nanny," he added, "a young French nanny."

"Why a French nanny?" Brady asked.

"So you can learn French." Aunt Sandy beamed like everybody thought that was a good idea, which I could tell everybody didn't.

Uncle Brett said, "After lunch I'm going to pick her up at

the bus station in town. Who wants to go with me?"

"She couldn't come all the way here from France on a bus!" Cousin Adele said. I could tell she was deeply displeased with the whole idea by the way she said it.

"True. She flew from Quebec City, Canada, to Uncle Marc's city, where there's a big international airport. He picked her up and put her on the bus, and she's going to arrive right after lunch."

All during tuna fish sandwiches and leftover cupcakes, the cousins asked questions about her and what it was going to be like. She was nineteen. She had light brown hair. She had one older brother. Her name was Collette. Her parents were professors, and Uncle Brett had met them at a conference last spring. They were very nice people, and we were all going to learn a great deal about another culture.

Uncle Brett tried to explain how American children were disadvantaged by not knowing other languages and cultures. He wanted his family to be more cosmopolitan. Everybody was going to learn French. He'd spent a couple of years in France after he graduated from high school, and Aunt Sandy had taken a lot of French classes in university. It would be lots of fun. It was a great idea. We would all be happy. And the nanny would take over all the driving so Aunt Sandy could be the highly effective mayor she was capable of being.

It made better sense to me than it did to my cousins. But then, I'm used to change. I know how to look at something from inside out and upside down. Brady had no clue how to translate adult information into kid language where it made sense as to what you had to do next. I'd have to teach him new ways to see things.

At first everybody refused to go with Uncle Brett to get the nanny. Then Bits & Pieces said they wanted to go, which made the drive even more unpopular. Aunt Sandy said she'd like to show Ketchup & Mustard how to paint with their fingers on pretty white paper, so they backed out again.

Joaquin said he remembered hearing a church service in Latin once and it sounded really weird. Maybe French was weird-sounding too. So then it was only him and Carmen who wanted to be the first ones to hear what this foreign language sounded like. Then Aunt Sandy said that many French girls had a strong sense of fashion that was quite different from the American way, and then Adele thought she might be persuaded. It ended up that everybody except Grandma, Aunt Sandy, and Bacon & Eggs went to pick up the French nanny. I couldn't see how all of us would fit in the car if she had even one suitcase.

She had five suitcases and three shopping bags with stuff spilling out of them. Her English had a different sound to it, but she knew an awful lot of words, which was disappointing. Uncle Brett kept reminding her to please speak French; he wanted the authentic immersion experience for his children. Adele whispered to Carmen that Collette had a lot of fashion sense and to look at her scarves.

When we got back to the lake house, Adele was the one assigned to show the French nanny to her bedroom. Brady and Joaquin and Carmen and I hauled her stuff up the stairs as the two older girls walked on ahead.

I hadn't really noticed what Adele did all day before Collette came to live at the lake house, but now she spent every day absolutely gaga, following Collette around. She asked all kinds of questions about music and boyfriends and clothes and if Aunt Sandy or Uncle Brett were around, Collette would answer in French and then wink at Adele so the grown-ups couldn't see. I was sure that must mean something important, and I put on my sight-dog eyes.

Brady and I sort of snuck looks from various rooms. She was awfully pretty in a way I hadn't seen girls be pretty before. Her nose was too long, and her eyes were too big, and her hair was too stringy, and her clothes were strange lengths. But it all added up to absolutely beautiful. We couldn't take our eyes off her. When she spoke French we nearly collapsed with the beauty of it all.

I watched Brady, and I knew it was the same way with him as it was with me. It wouldn't do any good to talk about it, though. Obviously, neither one of us needed any help translating this event from adult language into kid language.

## NINETEEN

# END OF THE WORLD

The summer ended. It had to because the earth keeps turning and that's the nature of things. Brady and I never gave the end of summer a thought. You don't get sad about losing what you expect to happen again the next summer and the next summer and the next summer after that. It's the for-sure finish that makes you sad.

When his parents were driving Joaquin and me to meet the bus that would take us back to Aunt Amy's to begin school, Brady began punching me on the arm. I tried to punch him back before he could punch me back. And that went on for the twenty miles from the lake house to the bus stop in town. We were truly friends.

Joaquin and I gave Aunt Amy big hugs when we saw her and tried to tell her about the summer, but we couldn't tell the hundredth part of it. There was too much, and it was too happy. I would still be trying to hunt down the right words if I'd ever tried to tell it all.

School began with me in fifth grade and Joaquin in first. My teacher already knew before we arrived that Aunt Amy was our legal guardian. It was kind of strange and wonderful to be going back to a building that was familiar, full of teachers and friends I already knew. Joaquin thought school was the next best thing to summers at the lake house with cousins.

There was food on the table morning and night, and Aunt Amy took us to visit interesting places on Sunday afternoons when the store was closed. But I could feel something in the air. Something uneasy. Something that set me to worrying, even in my sleep.

Finally I realized it was Aunt Amy I should worry about. I knew she could see something bad was about to happen. But try as I would, I couldn't get her to tell me what to look for.

October had just begun when Aunt Amy's world came crashing down. She lost the lease for the store. I didn't know this could happen to a good store owner who paid her bills and earned money from her work.

The people who owned the building had sold it, and the new owners wanted to turn the whole thing into a big restaurant, not little shops. The other little shop owners found other places to rent, but Aunt Amy had no savings, and she was low on working capital because of Momma's bills. There was no way she could come up with a down payment on a new lease, the rent money, new merchandise, and interior decorating for a new space all at once.

She applied for a bank loan from Uncle Marc's friend but

got turned down when they found out her last quarter earnings were low and that she had two dependents. That meant Joaquin and me. She called Uncle Brett, but he didn't have any extra money. Even though Aunt Sandy had just started her new job as mayor of the town, they had a lot of debts left over from graduate school and the babies.

Aunt Amy called Uncle Marc. He said the economic downturn had left him as strapped for cash as she was. Some of his investments had completely bottomed out.

Aunt Amy started to panic. She yelled at him, "Does that mean you're going to lose your law practice? Does that mean you're going to lose each of your three luxury cars? Will you have to sell your house? Are your kids going to have to drop out of school and take jobs at the local factory?"

Whatever Uncle Marc was saying on the other end wasn't helping.

"Well that's what no cash flow means to me, you pompous so-and-so!" She started to cry into the phone and after a little while hung up without saying good-bye. He didn't call back. I watched the mail every day to see if a letter with a check inside would come. None did.

At night Joaquin and I would try to imagine where we were going to live, what was going to happen to all of us. Finally I couldn't stand the tension and I started to pester Aunt Amy to tell me what was going to happen. That's when I discovered she didn't know. She didn't have a clue. No plan at all.

That was the second most scared I've ever been. Aunt Amy was the lady who believed in plans. If she didn't have one, then her world must be coming to an end.

I worked on the problem over and over in my mind. I'd try out all kinds of plans on Joaquin. He thought I had taken to telling him bedtime stories and was enjoying it. So I kept on telling him my imaginary plans every night.

Finally, Aunt Amy had no choice but to sell off everything in the store. She paid a lot of money to advertise all her merchandise for a huge going-out-of-business sale and said she needed our help. Joaquin and I were going to have to change schools anyway, so we quit a few weeks early to help her out during this hard time.

I will never understand why the happiest times of my life zip by like lightning and the saddest times trudge by so slowly that I can examine every miserable kink and bend in the day. Every time I'd put a bottle of perfume in a box, every time I'd see the last swish of a beautiful dress I recognized, I'd imagine I was saying good-bye to it. Joaquin didn't get that part so much. He simply liked all the activity going on around us.

That night I was making up a story for Joaquin about how great our lives were going to turn out when I realized that what I was inventing could really happen. I was startled by the possibility and could hardly let myself go to sleep, for fear I'd forget the happy ending during the night. It was still there when I woke up, thank goodness.

It was Saturday morning and Aunt Amy's liquidation sale was over. I watched how she buttered the toast at breakfast time with no attention to the dry edges. How she could hardly swallow her mint tea, which is usually her favorite.

How she didn't even tie the belt on her bathrobe. It was time to try out my newest bedtime story about how all our lives turned out happy.

"Aunt Amy," I said. "Let's call Uncle Brett and ask him if we could move into the lake house and take care of Grandma. I don't think Uncle Marc and Aunt Lana can be enjoying Grandma's company very much. I'll bet Uncle Marc would be really glad to have the offer."

Aunt Amy sat still for the longest time. Then she looked at me and her eyes softened for the first time in weeks. She said, "That's the best plan I've heard in a long time, Cheyenne."

She phoned Uncle Brett immediately, and in no time it was all arranged. We were moving back to the lake house!

Everybody seemed happy we were going to help Grandma live an independent life. I was right: Uncle Marc and Aunt Lana were about ready to send Grandma to a home for old people who can't take care of themselves. With us doing the job, it would cost a lot less, Uncle Marc said, and Aunt Amy probably needed a break from all the stress she'd been under this last year.

In a way it was kind of funny to hear Uncle Marc talk about the plan because he made it sound like he had thought of it. But Joaquin and I will always know that it was my plan and that it started out as a bedtime story.

## TWENTY

# THE LAKE HOUSE

The next morning we began packing: clothes, dishes, books, pictures off the wall, groceries in the cupboards, sheets and blankets, clothes, lamps. Everything. This was a whole new idea about moving. When Momma had moved, she announced it five minutes before it happened. She was always in such a hurry to go that we left behind everything but our clothes. If all of my stuff didn't fit in a suitcase I could carry, not all of it got to come.

But not Aunt Amy. Moving went on and on for days. It was a lot of hard work for all of us. Finally we loaded up her van to the top with boxes, strapped all three of us in the two front seats (which I personally know to be illegal), and started out for the lake house.

As we were driving across a long straight stretch one day, Aunt Amy began talking about some of her experiences. She said that the one thing she was most proud of in her life was that she had paid everybody the money she owed them before she closed the doors on her business. She had not gone bankrupt. She had had the dignity of paying her debts.

I reached under the seat belt with one arm and hugged her around the shoulders. Joaquin leaned forward past me to smile at her. It was the honest thing to do, he said. We were both proud of her.

I'll always remember the van Aunt Amy drove because it was the one she used to carry around all the clothes and supplies for her store. She had two seats for it, but you couldn't see the back one because it was so piled high with boxes of our moving stuff.

"You know how we got to keep this van?" she said, smiling, and patting the dashboard with her hand. "I got to keep this van because I paid all my debts. I own it. Nobody can come and say it's theirs. That's a good feeling, boys!" She drove a few minutes and then said, "Good old Noble Heart—that's what we should call this van!"

"Why?" Joaquin asked. We thought it was funny to name a car.

"Because its little engine just keeps on going, no matter how poor I am."

"I think we should call it Scuffy," he said.

Aunt Amy protested, laughing. "It's not so scuffy. It's just old and gentle."

I said, "If it makes it to the Lake House, it gets to be called Noble Heart, but if it breaks down, we have to call it Scuffy."

"Deal," she said, and we all shook each other's hands. Aunt Amy was the happiest I'd seen her in months. That whole trip she smiled and laughed and told us stories about when she was a little girl at the lake house. All along the way we made plans for how our life in the lake house would be, and when we drove up to the front door, I said, "Okay. Noble Heart got us here."

As we unpacked and began our new life, it wasn't at all like it had been in the summer-time. Everything was a little sadder and a little harder. The lake was rougher, the air was colder, and the garden was shaggy. Emptiest of all, the cousins weren't there. The house and yard held ghosts of last-summer cousins.

And Grandma wasn't just a dear old thing who got all our names wrong. She was stubborn and did dangerous things without realizing it. We couldn't let her out of our sight for one instant. She was as bad at making messes as Salt & Pepper.

Aunt Amy had to drive us twenty miles into town for school night and morning because we couldn't get bussing until we had lived there for a few months. Aunt Amy said we had to establish the lake home as our permanent residence first. That meant we had to load Grandma up in the van and take her with us into town every single day. Sometimes she wouldn't get in the car and we'd be late for school.

I hadn't noticed before this that the lake house didn't have a TV, but I sure noticed it now. I asked Aunt Amy why Grandma didn't have one. She said that a long time ago when I was born, my grandpa still had one, a small, old TV with a black and white picture. After Grandpa died, the family said Grandma needed a new one. She said, "No, I don't." She got rid of the old TV and turned the room off the kitchen into a reading room with bookshelves and lamps and little tables.

Joaquin asked, "So are we supposed to call it a reading room?"

Aunt Amy said, "Well, what do you do in that room?"

"Read," he said.

"Do homework," I said.

"Well then?" Aunt Amy laughed and flopped down in a big chair. She pulled Joaquin onto her lap, even though he was way too big to cuddle now. But probably his heart needed the snuggle, because he kind of burrowed into her. It was kind of funny looking, the two of them, because his new school shoes made his feet look even more enormous. I had to think about his feet because I wished with every inch of me that I wasn't so old and could have a snuggle like that sometimes.

Aunt Amy asked me to choose a picture book from the shelves that lined the room. I pulled over the other big, soft chair until it was touching Aunt Amy's and then she read to us. Joaquin and I can both read our own stories, of course, but we love the way Aunt Amy changes her voice for each character and how she makes the story extra exciting by the way she says the words.

After school one day I asked Aunt Amy if I could phone Brady. I really missed him. She said okay. Brady said his family was coming to the lake house for Thanksgiving Day, same as always, and his birthday was the day after. That gave Joaquin and me something big to look forward to.

I tried to think of what I could give Brady for a present.

I picked up a couple of snail shells from the lake shore that were very large and I collected all the different kinds of pine cones that had dropped since summer. I was planning on gluing them on the inside of a cereal box that I had cut into flat pieces, but when I laid them all out, it didn't look very pretty.

I worried about it for awhile and then asked Aunt Amy if she had any ideas how we could make a nice birthday present for Brady. She did. We needed a couple of balloons, some masking tape, string, a bowl of water, a few cups of flour, and all the newspapers from last summer that were still stacked in the back entrance. Joaquin helped me gather everything we needed.

Aunt Amy showed us how to rip the newspapers in long strips about an inch wide. We blew up the balloons and taped the small one to the big one to make an animal shape. We mixed the flour with some water in the large bowl and began dipping the paper strips into the wet mixture and slapping them gently against the balloons. Aunt Amy called it papier-mâché. We were making a piñata to fill with interesting things like the pine cones and shells I had collected, plus some candy and bubble gum from the store.

Finally Thanksgiving vacation came around, and the lake house was full of cousins again. Brady was really excited about the papier-mâché animal gift and shook it a little to hear all the rustling inside. He got to decide what kind of an animal it was going to be—that was part of his birthday present. He said it was a bear.

All the cousins cut up little pieces of green and yellow

and blue crepe paper that Brady's mom had brought with her. Then we glued them wherever Brady told us to. He got to draw the little black bear eyes and nose and mouth with black marking pen. Then we let it sit and dry for all of Thanksgiving Day.

The next day was his birthday. I knew what was going to happen. Part of having a piñata at your party is hanging it from a tree and batting it open with a big stick so you can get to the candy. I was feeling pretty bad about breaking something I'd worked so hard to make, so Aunt Amy took my picture with the piñata when nobody was watching. That way I could always remember it full of treats and not smashed open on the ground. It helped a lot.

Uncle Brett was really tricky about pulling the rope up and down when we were swinging at it, so it took us a lot of swings to finally connect. Wham! All the treats spilled out and everybody scrambled around on the flat limp grass to pick them up. Stop & Go were very good at picking things up off the ground, even if they hadn't been in the piñata. They caused Adele a lot of work.

Brady and I became expert at finding animal holes in the ground, now that the grass wasn't so perky. We thought the animals that lived in the holes would pop their heads out and look at us if we were able to keep very still. Usually it was only gophers. They were almost as impatient as we were and couldn't stand waiting underground.

One of my favorite times was when Cousin Bill and his friends played kick ball with us. They laughed and joked around with us, which made it lots of fun. We were divided into two teams, but it wasn't really soccer. I liked that they never did tall-kids-against-short-kids. They mixed us up so that Brady and I were never on the same team and there were an even number of big and little people on each team.

I loved seeing how fast the high school boys could move. We shorter kids didn't hold back. We were running as hard as we could, trying to trip them and grab for the ball with our hands. We even lunged after their shirts billowing by.

Bill and his friends probably could have hurt us a lot if they'd really gone all out to win, but none of them ever tried to trip us or shove us out of the way. It was very interesting to watch how they were playing by rules, but we weren't. It gave me a few ideas about how I wanted to be when my legs were that long.

## TWENTY-ONE

# CHRISTMAS

Aunt Amy loved Christmas. She was as happy then as Momma had been with her handsome boyfriend when the butterfly of true love had landed on her shoulder. We played special Christmas music all day long. One evening we decorated a tree and before we went to bed Aunt Amy told us the Christmas story. I hadn't known about any of that before. It was all very magical and adventurous.

Grandma spent the rest of the days before Christmas taking the ornaments off the tree. She had a big stash of large-size safety pins in her apron pocket that she used to redistribute the ornaments around the house. As soon as she'd pin one on a curtain, she'd call one of us to come and see how beautiful it looked. Many of the prettiest ones were made of glass or had pokey metal parts on them. We had to be careful where we stepped or sat, because the ornaments could be anywhere.

In only a few days the tree was bare and Grandma said

it was so sad Christmas was over and we'd have to throw out the tree. She picked up the tree—electric lights and tree-top star and all—and chucked it out the door. She was very strong and none of us could stop her. Well, Aunt Amy didn't try very hard, I thought.

Aunt Amy said to let Grandma enjoy her Christmas and not to scold her. We would gather the ornaments together and bring the Christmas tree back into the house on Christmas Eve so that Grandma could celebrate all over again.

Aunt Amy helped Joaquin and me put on a little play for the cousins when they arrived. We wore costumes we put together out of leftover clothes we found in the closets all over the house. I knew something about plays and pageants from being at school. My attendance was something the teachers could never count on, though, so I had never been given anything to do in a school play except stand in the back and wish I was the kid with a real costume.

This time I had a costume. And a real part where I had to memorize lines. Joaquin had lines to memorize too. For some reason, he decided they had to be yelled. I don't know what gave him that idea. Everybody laughed, of course, so then he kept on shouting until the end of the play. Aunt Amy stood by and started the music whenever the play was supposed to have some. At the end, everybody clapped. Joaquin and I took hands and bowed. We had done a good job.

Brady said our play was cool and asked Aunt Amy if she'd make up a play for all the cousins next year. Her eyes were all bright and glistening when she promised him yes, she would.

Momma had usually had a boyfriend at Christmas time, which was an expensive project, so we didn't usually have money for a tree or anything. That year we had more presents under the tree than I'd ever seen before. The cousins brought us presents too. Aunt Amy said our present to them was the pageant.

On Christmas morning, Joaquin and I tiptoed down the stairs and sat on the landing above the great room where the stairs change direction. The house was very quiet because we were the first ones up—even before Brady and Carmen. I told Joaquin we needed to sit on the stairs and memorize how everything looked because it was so beautiful.

I asked him what he liked best about Christmas, and he said, "Waiting."

"Waiting for what?"

"Nothing. Because you don't know what's in the presents or anything. All of it is fun because it's the waiting." He wasn't saying it exactly, but I knew what he was thinking inside. I told him I liked the waiting too. The waiting is what I will always remember about that Christmas morning. In the waiting we could smell the pine tree and hear the cousins waking up excited all over the big house. We sniffed the cinnamon coming from the kitchen oven where pull-apart rolls with pecans and cherries were baking.

I didn't want the clock in the living room to keep on ticking because I knew soon the room would change. The presents inside the wrappings would be things we'd seen on TV or in the store. But right then, during the waiting, they were hidden and magical.

In a few minutes Brady came running down with Carmen close behind him. After that, there was a whole flood of people, and I got washed into the Christmas room along with them. The wrapping paper began to fly through the air and everybody wore the ribbons around their necks and stuck the bows in their hair. Brady put a big red velvet poinsettia bow right on top of his dad's head, and his dad left it there. It looked partly silly and partly pretty.

Aunt Amy gave Joaquin his very own game board of Chinese checkers with beautiful clear glass marbles. She gave me a collection of card games that had all sorts of different pictures and a booklet of instructions so that you could play six or ten different games just by changing the rules.

Before we went to bed that night Joaquin said, "I'm putting my Chinese Checkers in my backpack to keep it safe. Are you?"

I didn't even have to think about it twice. "Me too," I said. We moved some of his food hoard into my bag because his game was bigger than my cards. We had to shake the bags a few times to make things settle, but finally we got it all to fit and zippered the bags shut.

The next day, Aunt Amy came into our bedroom to see if we were awake yet. She had important news, she said. I clenched myself together. I didn't like the sound of that.

Sure enough, it was terrible. We'd be moving again. Right away.

Aunt Amy could see I was really seized up about it and began to explain more. About a month ago Uncle Marc had called to say he and Aunt Lana wanted to have a big party for their children's friends at the lake house. It was supposed to be a real old-fashioned type of New Year's party with guests sleeping over and the party lasting for a few days. His plan was for Grandma to go visit her sister in a nearby city and for the three of us to move to a cottage the family owned on the other side of the lake.

I asked Aunt Amy why she had waited so long to tell us.

She said, "Because you didn't need to know. Now was soon enough." Well, that was fair, I guessed. "It would have just laid a lot of worry over the top of Christmas," she added.

I think there was another reason Aunt Amy had waited so long to tell us the news. She wasn't saying, but I knew what it was. Aunt Amy was pleased to have a plan. Holding close an important secret like that made her feel responsible and secure and very much in charge of us all.

After breakfast Brady and I walked with Aunt Amy and Uncle Brett around the lake to take a look at this cottage. In the summer the family rented it out to tourists who wanted to visit the area for a short while. It was a little spidery and cold inside, but I liked it all the same. There were two great big rooms. One had a fireplace with sofas in front of it and a kitchen and a big table at the other end. The other room had two bunk beds against one wall, a big bed against the other wall, and a bunch of dressers and cabinets in between.

That side of the lake didn't have regular power connections, so Uncle Brett showed Aunt Amy how the generator worked and I watched very carefully, being a sight dog as always. We left the summer cottage warming up by itself and little by little over the next few days we moved our things into it.

The cousins thought the cottage was a cool place, and I think Brady may have been a little jealous he didn't get to live there.

## TWENTY-TWO

# RUNAWAY

We had only four more days of Christmas vacation to play together before the cousins had to go home and Joaquin and I would start living in the summer cottage with Aunt Amy. It snowed almost every day and time suspended like we were in another world. Silence outside, where sound ended in the fall of snowflakes; noise inside, where sound bounced off walls decorated with holly wreaths. A white and snowy cocoon world with a leathery brown world snuggled inside it. Every part of me felt comfortable. My mind slept at night and my body was gentle in the day. Even my elbows and knees felt soft.

Brady and I would often curl into the listening place we had discovered in the corner of the stairs. It was a perfect place for eavesdropping on people's conversations. The only problem with it being behind the bend of the stairs is that we never got the beginning, the middle, and the end of any conversation. It was always just little snippets passing by. I was listening for information on Dead Uncle Dick, as always, but nobody had anything to say about him.

We both nearly died every time Collette said anything in any language. Brady punched my arm and I punched him back every time she walked by.

The day Brady's family was supposed to leave, Brady and I stayed in our stair-bend hiding place long after Uncle Brett had sounded his fourth "Last call for the Brett and Sandy Walker Family." We watched him search the house and flush out all the children, including the nanny. Finally Brady burst out of our hiding place. Uncle Brett grinned and grabbed him and pretended to swat his rear end, but he didn't really do it.

Brady and I weren't sad to see each other go this time either. He would come for Easter, of course, and we planned out how we were going to beg for a couple of visits in between. Then the overloaded car drove off, and Joaquin and I helped Aunt Amy get the house ready for Uncle Marc's family's party. We did a really good job and the whole place was shining, top to bottom. It felt really good to work that hard.

I guess the New Year's party was a great success. We could hear the music and noise from across the lake at night, but we weren't invited to attend any of it. Before they left, though, Uncle Marc drove over to the summer cottage and told Aunt Amy that Grandma would be staying with her sister for a few weeks longer or perhaps until spring. At any rate, the family would appreciate it if she would come over to the lake house at least two or three times a week: open it up, dust, clean, vacuum, check for leaks and mice, and generally keep it livable. His children and their friends had loved the time they had just spent there, and their family anticipated using the lake house again soon. He was sure Brett and his family felt the same way.

Aunt Amy said, "Sure, fine," and looked in the other direction.

I could see her point. Uncle Marc was an okay kind of person, but everything was about himself and his little family. He'd drawn too small a circle. I thought his family circle should have included all of us: aunts, uncles, and cousins. But if Aunt Lana could only be happy with a very small circle, I wondered if Uncle Marc had any other choice. I asked Aunt Amy about this. She pursed her lips and didn't make an answer, but I had the feeling she thought exactly the same way I did.

School began again, and we had to leave extra early in the morning so we could all help shovel the snow where it had drifted across the road. I hated to miss even part of a day at school because I always felt like I was a little behind. My grades were good. Really good, in fact. The feeling I had was that I didn't quite feel prepared. Ever. I worried that something might whip by me and I'd miss it.

The flu started going around the school but it didn't whip by us, that's for sure. Joaquin got it first. Then I got it. And then Aunt Amy got it. Her flu was worse than ours. I don't know why. She ached everywhere and could hardly move. She couldn't even drive us to school because she was too weak to shovel any snow at all.

Joaquin and I knew quite a few of her cooking recipes by then, so we took very good care of her. But the snow was high, and it was very cold outside. She told us not to check on the lake house without her. It could wait a few days.

But Grandma couldn't.

Grandma couldn't wait until spring came to be back in her lovely lake house. We found out later how it happened. One morning when Grandma's sister had gone out for groceries, Grandma saw a taxi pull up in front of the apartment building. She put on her hat and coat, grabbed her handbag, and told that taxi driver where she wanted to go. He must have been delighted with the fare he was going to collect for that long a drive and they set out.

Once she got to the lake house Grandma couldn't remember how to turn the heat up. There was no food in the fridge. Everything in the cupboards was kept in plastic because of the mice, and her fingers couldn't undo the ziplock bags. Sometime within the next twenty-four hours, Grandma had a stroke and died instantly. But we didn't know any of that for a couple of days.

When Aunt Amy was mostly over the flu, we all walked over to the lake house to dust and sweep up a bit. We opened the door and saw Grandma lying on the floor, cold. Aunt Amy is not the screaming type, but she screamed then. So did I. So did Joaquin. But there was no one but ourselves to hear us scream.

We carried Grandma into the bedroom but we couldn't get her to lie flat. It was awful to see, the way her body was twisted up like she was still lying on her tummy on the floor, one knee up and to the side. Just awful.

I turned up the heat. Aunt Amy got on the phone and called her brothers. Things were starting to get confusing, so Joaquin took some crackers out of the plastic seal and spread some peanut butter and jelly on them. He handed round the plate very carefully. Maybe it sounds heartless, like we didn't care. But no matter how sad your heart might be, your tummy always shouts louder.

It took the ambulance a long time to get out to the lake house through the snow drifts. But maybe they didn't hurry. There was no use, of course. They didn't have on their lights or sirens when they came, just pulled up like any old van. The men walked across the carpet with their clompy boots and took Grandma away. Joaquin asked them to turn on their whirling lights for us when they left, but they didn't.

## TWENTY-THREE

# FUNERAL

The day before the funeral, Aunt Sandy and all the children, plus Collette, arrived in a brand-new van. Uncle Brett was coming later in their old car after work. Any other time I would have wanted to sit with Brady in his new car and pretend to drive, but I had an important job to keep up. Listening. I didn't even know what to listen for, but I had the feeling things had changed. I couldn't let myself be a carefree kid for even a minute.

Brady noticed I was different and kept watching me. But what could I tell him? That something was there, in the air around us, something that everybody but the kids knew about, but nobody was mentioning? I could see the stiffness, the words that weren't quite right, the hugs where people didn't really touch, the trying to get it right when everything was somehow wrong.

The more the family gathered, the worse it got. Sometimes I would feel so tense I'd take Joaquin and hide under the bed in the loft beside the ladder-stairs. I wanted to just plain disappear. Besides, it was a perfect place to hear everything going on in one big room of the house without being seen. But Joaquin's sense of self-preservation wasn't as keen as mine. He'd make the excuse that he had to go pee. I knew he wanted to play with Carmen. They didn't pay nearly the attention to grown-ups that they should. When this was all over, I'd have to teach Joaquin how to be a better sight dog.

The day of the funeral was cold and grey, which meant a lot of people didn't want to go outside and were stuffed into the lake house. If we had gone to school that day we would have had a Valentine's Day party with cupcakes and red cinnamon hearts. Give you two guesses where I'd rather have been.

It was even more crowded at the lake house because Aunt Lana said this was an "entirely unplanned event" and her family had books to read and papers to write for their classes. She posted the reading room beside the kitchen as a quiet zone. Rough & Tumble didn't even dare go in there.

The funeral was held at the church in the town about half an hour away from the lake house. This church did not have men wearing beautiful costumes, nor were there big swaying incense burners, pouring smoke. It was a much quieter church with a few singers and a small organ to make the music. Lots of people spoke about Grandma, how she had been as a school girl, and as a mother, and as a friend. I gathered that she had been a really happy person and that everybody liked her a lot. That was nice to know.

I asked Aunt Amy about this on the way back to the lake house. She was quiet for a little while and then said, yes, it was all true, and that sometimes seeing a person another way helps make your own way of seeing more complete. That made sense to me.

We brought all the flowers back to the lake house with us. I'd never been completely surrounded by flowers before. The air smelled delicate and sweet, and I imagined what it would be like to live inside a flower bed. I decided to try it out. If I moved the large containers around just so, I could sit in the middle of them without anybody knowing I was there. But Uncle Brett saw me anyway. He came over and sat down by the flowers and waited for me to say something, but I didn't. I couldn't. Then he moved a big pot and slid over to where I was curled up with my arms around my knees.

After a while he said that he knew Grandpa and Grandma were together now. I liked that idea very much. I asked him what he thought they'd be doing. He said they'd be going for a walk and holding hands and telling jokes. I asked what they'd be saying to each other. He said they'd be talking about the things they cared about the most: their children and grandchildren.

I asked Uncle Brett how Grandma would know what to tell Grandpa, since her mind hadn't been working very well when she left the world. He said that her body was young and pretty again and her mind was whole and well. I asked what she would look like and he took out a large picture album from when she was a pretty lady like Momma, when my momma was her baby. The more he talked to me about Grandma, the less I felt like hiding and crying.

Brady poked his head in and started to look at the picture albums with us. I wished then that I was his brother and not his cousin. But I'm okay with it now.

## TWENTY-FOUR
# FAMILY COUNCIL

Promptly after breakfast, Uncle Marc called a family meeting for the adults. I wasn't even surprised this time. Joaquin and I glanced at each other with our special signal. We made our bodies even and smooth and slow as we made our way around the edges of the big room. Brady almost caught us, but we leaned back out of the light until he left. We climbed the ladder-stairs as smoothly as we could. It's the jerking motions adults pick up on.

I kind of jumped when I saw somebody lying on one of the beds. It was Cousin Bill and he appeared to be taking a nap. His eyes were closed and he didn't say anything to us. I looked at Joaquin, and he knew I was telling him to be especially silent sliding under the bed next to the ladder-stairs.

After we were in position under the bed, I made Joaquin promise that he'd stay. I really needed him to hear what was happening so that after when we talked it over I'd be able to remember for sure what I'd heard and not get it mixed up with what I'd imagine I'd heard. If you're scared enough, the two get rolled up together, and on your own you can't ever separate them. They might even talk about Dead Uncle Dick again.

Uncle Marc cleared his throat and said, "I know I speak for the entire family when I say that the occasion that prompts this meeting has been especially difficult for every one of us."

He paused. I think he was probably looking at each person individually. That was a habit of his. It was designed to make any guilt in your soul well up and pour out of you so that you'd confess your crime and save him a lot of trouble telling you what your crime was.

Then he said, "Amy, after due consideration, we have decided not to press charges of criminal neglect."

I heard her gasp and say, "What?"

Uncle Brett said, "What do you mean? This is the first I've heard anything of the sort."

Aunt Lana said, "You really have no idea how difficult it is, having people accuse us behind our backs of neglecting Mother. It's been the most humiliating, awful experience of my life." She began to sniffle. "Imagine Mother coming into this house, all cold and shut up, and counting on Amy's help. Then, when she needed it most, when we have all paid for the help to be there, the help was not there." She said the last three words all slow and solemn. Then Aunt Lana's sniffle turned into weeping, and I could see imaginary faces in her social circle nodding to each other and whispering.

Aunt Sandy said, "But Amy was very sick. Too sick to

leave her bed. Besides, none of us knew Mother was even at the cottage."

Aunt Lana's voice was muffled. "Exactly my point," and she sobbed some more.

Uncle Marc wanted control and cleared his throat. "Precisely. No one knew. No one knew who should have known. The arrangements Lana and I made for Mother were impeccable. But neither Mother's sister nor Mother's daughter knew where she was."

Uncle Brett said very loudly, "Those accusations are unfair and unfounded. We've experienced a sad event in our family, but it's no tragedy, and it's no one's fault. Now get on with the will so we can all go home . . . and . . . get on with things."

His ending was a little weak, I thought. Maybe he was susceptible to one of Uncle Marc's stares. We heard bumping sounds and then two snaps as Uncle Marc opened his briefcase. He talked about how there wasn't much money left in their mother's account. I knew it! That's why he was so glad Aunt Amy would work for so cheap.

He said, "A sixth share amounts to . . ." and then there were a lot of numbers I couldn't keep track of without a pencil.

We heard Aunt Amy say, "And what about the rest of Coco's hospital bills?"

"Yes, yes, we'll get to that."

"Get to it now," Aunt Amy demanded.

"If you insist, here is the paperwork for liquidating a portion of the boys' trust fund in lieu of their mother's needs."

"You can't dip into Cheyenne and Joaquin's trust fund! That was set up for their education, for their start in life. How can that even be legal?"

"Are you officially requesting legal interpretation? I'm sure I can help you find someone you can trust where legal issues are concerned since you're clearly displeased with the pro bono services I've been offering," Uncle Marc said stiffly.

Brett said, "Come on, Marc. This isn't how a family is supposed to treat one another! She's just shocked that everything has changed. Why weren't we told?"

Uncle Marc ignored him. "On another matter, I had a discussion with Dick a while ago, and the subject of the family's lake house came up . . ."

I nudged Joaquin. "Hear that?"

"Yeah," he said. "I gotta pee."

"Don't think about it. Shhhhh!"

"You mean this house?" Aunt Sandy was asking.

"Yes." Uncle Marc paused, and I knew he must be looking over his glasses at her. That was a look he'd probably designed to make people in court yell out how they really didn't know anything anymore. Not what they'd seen, not what they'd heard, and they were no longer even sure of their own names.

"It seems to us that we may be able to find a better investment return on our money than this piece of real estate if we consider world markets."

Nobody said anything at all. Maybe they were in shock. It's for sure I was. I couldn't imagine anything more valuable than the good times we cousins had had at the lake house. It was ours. It belonged to all of us. Money didn't come into any of that.

Then Uncle Marc began again. He was reading another list of numbers, and I found it difficult to follow. If I'd had a paper and pencil with me, I could have kept track of what he was talking about, maybe, but my mind was clogged up with a lot of information already.

Then everybody was talking at once, and I started to feel drowsy, like if I curled up really tightly in a ball I could close out the world. Like I could drift into a deep hibernating sleep where I'd only wake up again if the spring promised to be wonderful and if Brady would be coming to the lake house for Easter.

Finally I heard Aunt Amy's voice over the rest. She was speaking very loudly and clearly. "I can see how things are going. How long do the boys and I have in the summer cottage before you'll want to rent it out?"

Uncle Marc said, "Yes, that opens up another subject, Amy. It seems to us—"

Uncle Brett was practically shouting, "What do you mean by 'us'? Who on earth is that? It's not me! It's not Sandy. I'm darn sure it isn't Amy. Tell us, Marc, who is 'us'?"

Marc went right on like Uncle Brett hadn't said a thing.

"—that there is a pressing need for the family to provide other care for Coco's children. Clearly Amy is unable to care even for herself. She has no job, she has no education or training. Do we want to continue Coco's irresponsible upbringing of the boys with that of Amy's? We have approached Dick on the subject. Certainly the boys have the right to a more stable family life than she can provide. Dick may—"

Aunt Amy screamed, "You can't do this to me, Marc. You can't! You can't take those boys away from me. They're my life! Besides, I'm their guardian."

"Actually, you are no longer their legal guardian. That order was time-dated and has been rescinded as of . . ." and I could hear him shuffling papers that would provide the exact date, as if that mattered at all at this point.

There was a dead silence in the living room. My heart was thumping so loud inside me that I couldn't hear anything else for awhile. Then over the top of it I heard Aunt Amy crying.

A chair scraped and Aunt Sandy's firm voice said, "Marc, Lana, Amy. We have enjoyed loving relationships in this family for too long to be torn apart by differences now. I formally request that you, Marc, send to each member of the family a copy of all the documents that you have referred to today. We would like to see a written discussion, free of all legal jargon, briefly outlining all your recommendations. We will review them and we will reconvene here as a family as soon as we can contact Dick and Lotta. All in favor, raise your hand."

I had my head in my arms and didn't see that part. I assume everybody's hands went up. Aunt Sandy would make a very good mayor, I could tell. I was just starting to think about the uncles contacting Dead Uncle Dick when I heard the bed next to us creak. I had forgotten about Bill lying there, probably listening to the whole thing like Joaquin and me. I felt sorry for him, hearing his dad say stuff like that. I couldn't let him know we were there. Sad things like that need to be private. So I put my hand on Joaquin's arm to keep him still until Bill had gone and the room below sounded empty. We crawled out just in time to see Uncle Marc and Aunt Lana and the three tall cousins drive away in their sleek black car.

## TWENTY-FIVE
# SLEEPOVER

So much had happened that it seemed like years had passed. Really it was only lunchtime. Aunt Sandy and Aunt Amy were doing their best to be normal, but I saw how hard Aunt Amy had to work to keep the anger and the grief stored up. Every time she looked out the kitchen window, the bad feelings would start to spill out and she'd have to grip the sink and push against them.

If I had been alone with her, pretty soon I'd have been the same way as she was, but Brady was not used to picking up on adult things like I was. He told me to get a grip. He said we needed to go exploring around the summer cottage after lunch and he didn't give two hoots that it was sleeting.

Uncle Brett said, "I'm afraid not. We've got to leave for home right after lunch."

Brady was desperate to sleep over at the summer cottage. He pointed out that today was only Friday. They still had all of Saturday and Sunday to get ready for school and work on Monday. He had a point. He begged and Carmen begged. Then Vinegar & Oil started to beg, only they didn't even know what they were begging for—they just liked the sound of it.

Aunt Sandy looked at Collette, who looked like she'd just gotten out of bed in time for lunch. Of course, that's how she mostly looked, so it was hard to tell. Aunt Sandy asked her if she'd be willing to drive the children home in the new van the next day. She perked up and said, "*Mon plaisir.*" All of a sudden Adele said she was dying for a sleepover and could she please, please stay with Aunt Amy and the boys.

I stole a glance at Joaquin and he was as surprised as I was. Adele never spoke to either of us unless commanded by an adult. We were practically in a lower category than Rough & Tumble, if that were possible.

Aunt Sandy asked Collette how she felt about that. Collette yawned and stretched and said, "*Mais oui,*" as sweetly as possible. Brady and I nearly melted under the table.

Uncle Brett said they would be taking Vigor & Vim with them, so Collette would only have to handle three. Adele sat up very tall and tossed her hair. "I'll help Collette handle the younger children," she said.

"That would be just lovely," Aunt Amy said. "We'll have popcorn and we'll toast marshmallows in the fireplace."

"And tell ghost stories," Brady added.

I shot Joaquin another look. We weren't too keen on ghost stories, for reasons that you can imagine. When I asked Aunt Amy last year about ghosts that came back from the dead, she said she hated séances and that sort of thing and so did their whole family. I don't know if she's changed her mind or what, because in the family meeting this morning she hadn't objected to getting together with Dead Uncle Dick. Of course, Uncle Marc had thrown an awful lot in her direction, and she may have let the subject of one ghostly visit slip by her.

I had a lot of new information to think about. What if the family agreed with Uncle Marc that Aunt Amy couldn't have us anymore? That was an even bigger disaster than the plan about Dead Uncle Dick coming back. Even bigger than how the family was going to sell the lake house because of Momma's bills. Hearing adults make plans like that is enough to reduce your confidence in them as a group.

Before Uncle Brett left, he said to Aunt Amy, "How are you fixed for money?"

She said, "Am I being paid to take care of this house anymore?"

"Since Marc is all keen on making everything legal, and since he produced neither language nor papers to say you were fired, I believe you're still on the payroll."

Aunt Amy and Uncle Brett looked at each other then, and I saw how they felt about each other. It's good to know that Joaquin and I are like the people in our family. But sometimes it frightens me to love someone that much in case the person has to go away like Momma did.

Uncle Brett said, "Since you're picking up your mail in town at the post office, I'll call you when I get my copy of the papers from Marc's office. That way you'll know yours have probably arrived. Then we'll work together on how to handle things. Is that okay, little sister?"

Aunt Amy was close to tears and nodded her head. "Thanks."

Aunt Sandy took out her wallet and emptied everything she had into Aunt Amy's hand. "Here's a little cash to hold you over. Don't worry. We'll keep those deposits coming."

Aunt Amy wrapped her long arms around Sandy in a good-bye hug, and I saw her tears glistening on Aunt Sandy's hair. Aunt Sandy attempted to turn, but she was anchored by Yes & No hugging her legs. She smoothed their hair and gently peeled one of the twins off her body, handing him to Uncle Brett and snuggling the other.

After Uncle Brett's putt-around car drove off with the parents and twins inside, Aunt Amy sent everybody to the summer cottage to start playing board games. She asked Brady and me if we would help her clean up the lake house because we needed to leave it in top condition in case realtors started dropping by. I wondered why she didn't ask the two older girls, Collette and Adele, to do it. But I think Aunt Amy knew what kind of workers Brady and I would be.

To prove she was right, we worked as hard and as fast as we could. You wouldn't believe how quickly we had the place clean and shining. The only thing left to do was the bedding laundry and we had it all in piles, ready to begin the next day after everyone had gone home.

I asked Aunt Amy if we were going to stay in the summer cottage much longer. She didn't even ask how I knew it might be a problem. She just said she was going to look for work in town while Joaquin and I were in school all day. Then she asked me how I felt about it. I shrugged and said it seemed like a fine plan.

## TWENTY-SIX

# ICE STORM

That night the rain was bitterly cold and had begun to freeze on the trees as we drove around the lake to the summer cottage. Each twig was encased within a tube of glistening ice that winked and twinkled in the twilight. The woods took on an enchanted look of a colorless ice-crystal world, silver and black. Translucent trees stark in the fading afternoon sun.

When we walked in, we could hear Collette in the bedroom, talking in French on her cell phone, with the door closed. Adele was lounging on a sofa by the fire with a book, and Carmen and Joaquin were playing checkers on the dining table. After an hour when Collette still hadn't come out, Aunt Amy knocked quietly on the door. Collette was curled up on the bed, apparently having cried herself to sleep. I didn't know nineteen-year-old girls did that. I was quite sorry because I had wanted to go on believing Collette was enchanted.

After supper and games and stories, and then treats and games and stories, and then hot cocoa and games and stories, Aunt Amy said it was definitely bedtime. Our guests had a long drive the next day. Aunt Amy looked so tired herself, I thought she'd fall over in the doorway, but we had to sort out the beds first.

Aunt Amy suggested the girls sleep in the bedroom. She and Carmen would sleep in the big bed, and Collette and Adele could have the bunks. The three boys could sleep in the living room, with one person on an air mattress in front of the fireplace. It sounded good to me, but Collette said she couldn't sleep in a bunk. She would suffocate. She needed to be on a sofa in the living room with lots of air around her where she could watch the fire.

Then Adele said she needed to sleep on the other sofa in the living room. Collette wrinkled up her face at that, so then Adele had to say she really meant that she didn't want to sleep on the other sofa. We finally settled things with Collette exactly where she wanted to sleep—on the sofa in front of the fire. Whew!

It rained all night, I guess, but I didn't listen to it. Sleeping that close to a fire was like a sleeping potion to me. I missed everything I usually kept myself alert all night to hear. When we woke up in the morning Collette was gone. She had left a note, but it was in French.

Aunt Amy called her sister-in-law, who translated the letter despite Aunt Amy's mangled pronunciation. Apparently Collette had a boyfriend, and they were so in love they could no longer be parted. He had come to rescue her from her loveless plight in a foreign land, and she would soon be again in the arms of happiness. PS—the van would be in the parking lot of the city library.

That would put it right across the street from the bus depot. Handy. I thought she should have said something about being sorry she had run out on her duties and broken her word. That she hoped the children and family wouldn't suffer too much from her irresponsible behavior. Brady and I were very angry to be so disillusioned by beauty and romance all at the age of ten.

Uncle Brett and Aunt Sandy immediately began the drive back to the lake. The freezing rain had begun falling thick and heavy again, and it was going to be a long slow ride on slick, icy roads. Aunt Sandy picked up the van, and Uncle Brett returned to town in the car with Top & Bottom so the twins could fall asleep for an afternoon nap. He also needed to call his friends in Quebec City again to see if they'd heard anything from their daughter, Collette—a conversation that made him sad and embarrassed, he said. Aunt Sandy helped Adele, Brady, and Carmen pack up, and they left soon in the heavy van.

The summer cottage felt empty with just the three of us. But not for long. Forty minutes later, the big van pulled into our yard again. Aunt Sandy declared the roads impassable. Even the sanding trucks were in the ditch. She called Uncle Brett to tell him they were staying with us for another night. He said the twins were asleep, Collette had called her parents, and the freezing rain was slacking off the further he drove. He promised not to take any risks and to stay at a motel for the night if the roads became too dangerous.

The freezing rain continued to fall on the summer cottage all night. The trees groaned and shuddered with the weight. When a limb would snap, the ice falling all around sounded like panes of glass, shattering on our heads.

In the middle of it all, half asleep, I felt Aunt Amy shake my leg. "Cheyenne, are you awake?"

"Yes, the storm is too noisy to sleep."

"I think I'm in trouble," she said.

I was wide awake then. "What kind of trouble?"

"I don't know exactly, but I feel really strange. My head feels like someone's trying to yank it off my neck."

"What are you going to do?"

"I think I'd better go to the hospital and see what's wrong with me. My neck feels like it's being stretched up to the ceiling."

"But what about the storm?"

"I can't sit here and wait, Cheyenne. The way my body feels is really spooking me."

"What do I tell Aunt Sandy in the morning?"

"I think I'll be back in just a couple of hours. The doctor will give me some medicine and I'll be back before anybody knows I'm gone."

"What if you're not?"

"If I'm not . . ." Aunt Amy paused. Lies don't come natural to her like they do to some people. "Tell her I said to drop you and Joaquin off at the hospital. Tell her I've got a new cleaning job there. They called me in for an emergency because of the storm."

"Can you get to town on these roads?"

"I'll have to try, Cheyenne."

"Aunt Sandy couldn't do it."

"Not at the speed she likes to drive," Aunt Amy said, but her stretching neck must have made her too preoccupied to chuckle. I could see she was walking with her head high and stiff, not at all natural. "Tell Joaquin I expect you to take care of each other," she said.

"We always do."

"I know."

"Aunt Amy . . ."

"I have to go, Cheyenne . . ."

"We want to stay with you. Always." Sitting up, I hugged her around her knees.

"I want that too."

"Promise?"

"Promise."

She couldn't bend her head down to kiss me good-bye like usual, but she reached down with her fingers and messed my hair a little. And that's the last time I saw the happy, safe Aunt Amy.

## TWENTY-SEVEN
# LOST

In the morning Aunt Amy and her van were still gone. I told Aunt Sandy what Aunt Amy had told me to tell her. She looked worried and phoned Uncle Brett. The freezing rain had stopped, and Aunt Sandy said she wanted to try the roads. When she hung up, I pointed out that maybe she could drive really slowly. Brady looked at me funny, like he thought I was being a know-it-all. I shrugged and he smiled and punched my arm.

We hauled the tree limbs off the driveway onto the grass. One limb had fallen on the van. It was a smallish limb and the van had a good roof, so it only made a small dent. I didn't think it was worth noticing, but Aunt Sandy talked to Adele a lot about insurance. Adele was mostly interested in finding out news about Collette. If Aunt Sandy had any more information about Collette, she certainly wasn't giving it out freely.

I went back to lock up the summer cottage since I knew

where Aunt Amy hung the key. Just as I was pulling the
door closed, I thought of our book bags in the bottom of the
closet with our food hoard in them. I grabbed them both
and passed Joaquin his as I popped into the car. Just like
old times, he began protecting it to keep other people from
asking what was inside.

Aunt Sandy took a look at my stuffed and lumpy book
bag and congratulated me on being so careful about my stud-
ies. I didn't dare look at Brady. If this kind of thing kept on,
I wasn't sure if he'd want to be best cousin-friends with me
anymore.

As soon as we were on the main road, Aunt Sandy started
asking me questions like I knew things. I had to invent a
little bit. I said, "Aunt Amy got a job cleaning at the hospital.
Usually she will work days while Joaquin and I are at school,
but just this once they needed her to come in at night because
of the storm."

Joaquin heard the lie loud and clear and looked at me
sharply. I gave him the look that said, "I'll tell you later." The
thing about lies is that you have to live with them forever
after. As things turned out, it was the luckiest lie I could
have made up. For quite a while it covered everything we
needed to hide.

All the way to the hospital Aunt Sandy sang Aunt Amy's
praises. About what a hard worker she was. How the whole
family should be proud that she'd already gotten a secure
job at the hospital, with insurance and all sorts of benefits
thrown in, probably. I wasn't sure what that might include,
but it was one of those discussions you didn't want to continue

on your own. I just let Aunt Sandy play the whole thing out without any help from me. You save yourself a lot of trouble that way. Besides, Aunt Sandy didn't have to sell Joaquin and me on how great Aunt Amy was—we knew that better than anybody.

When we got to the hospital parking lot, we didn't see Aunt Amy's van, but I told Aunt Sandy she might have parked it at a friend's house. I reassured Aunt Sandy that everything was fine. We'd go wait on the bench in the front of the hospital until Aunt Amy's shift ended, which was going to be in half an hour.

When Aunt Sandy and the cousins pulled out, I felt alone and scared for Aunt Amy. And that was just the first speck of what I was going to keep on feeling for . . . well . . . I don't know how much longer it's going to be going on.

Once we were sure they had gone, Joaquin and I went searching for the van. We walked around some of the other parking lots nearby: the grocery store, the gas station, the city library, the bus stop. It wasn't in any of those places.

Then we saw people going into the hospital: whole families with grandmas and little kids. So when the next big group came along, Joaquin and I sort of attached ourselves at the end and walked right in, past all the people who kind of look you over. When you don't know what you're doing, you have to remember never to look at anyone directly and to always act like you're focused on going somewhere. Then people leave you alone, usually. This hospital was not large since it was not a large town. That was good, I thought, because we'd be able to find Aunt Amy quickly.

We began on the first floor and looked in every single bed up all three floors of the little hospital. We found rooms with children, rooms with old people, rooms of men, and rooms with mothers and brand-new babies, but not one of them held Aunt Amy.

"Do you think they're still working on her?" I asked Joaquin when we were back outside.

"They didn't do any kind of private work on Momma. She just lay in a bed and slept."

"Yes, but she had some tubes stuck in her, remember?"

"Oh, yeah. I forgot."

"Maybe it took them a long time to get Aunt Amy hooked up."

The street lights had come on while we had been searching the hospital, and they made the ice on the trees sparkle like a fairyland picture. But sometimes living inside the picture is a whole lot different than looking at it from the outside, like in a picture book. It was cold as can be and the air was wet from the ice storm. With the darkness coming, I began to feel scared about where we were going to spend the night.

I said, "Joaquin, we've got to find the van. So we have to think like Aunt Amy when she got to the hospital."

"How's that?"

"She was sick. Her head hurt. She said it felt like somebody was trying to pull her head off. She held it up really high and stiff."

"Poor Aunt Amy," he said and sounded like he might cry.

"You can't cry about her now. Help me think how she was thinking."

"Maybe she couldn't think."

"Yeah," I said, "like when you fall down and you don't even know you're in a mud puddle because you have to keep on doing what you were doing."

"Yeah, and she hurt so bad. Maybe she had her eyes closed and couldn't even see where she was going."

We stood in the parking lot behind the hospital, thinking about this. It was a big square building made out of red bricks with three layers of windows. Somewhere in there Aunt Amy was really, really sick and probably very scared. And outside Joaquin and I were really, really cold and for sure very scared.

"Okay, let's pretend we're Aunt Amy," I said. I took Joaquin's hand and we walked to the front of the hospital. I pointed out which road she had to take to drive into the hospital. There was only one choice. We stood looking at the front of the hospital. On the left side there was a sign that said "Emergency" and a place to drive up beside it like in front of a hotel.

All of a sudden I knew that was the door she had gone in. I just knew it. If she was having an emergency with her head about ready to pop off, she would have gone in that door. Then I saw that if she had missed her aim at the driveway by the emergency sign, she would have driven along a narrow gravel space off to the side that had a strip of grass beside it and then bushes and a wooden fence further over.

We crossed the street toward the hospital and walked

over to the narrow gravel alley to look. It was true. Someone had driven on the frozen grass and gravel because there were two lines of tire marks there. Unless two people rode their bikes in that spot. Except the tire marks were too wide and too deep for bicycles. A car had to have made those tracks.

"Come on," I said to Joaquin. "Let's see if these tire marks go further." We walked along, following them, until they disappeared inside a little forest at the back of the hospital beside the grocery store parking lot. We stepped into the woods, which were spooky in the dark. Then I saw it: a dim light.

Joaquin said, "I'm cold. Let's go inside the hospital. We could sleep on the big chairs." I knew he was scared of going further into the woods. So was I. It was pitch dark now, with no moon or anything.

"If the hospital people figure out we don't have a grown-up with us, they'll make us live with strangers, Joaquin. You know that's true."

"I know, but I'm scared."

"Let's see what's making the light," I said. I had been pulling on his arm to come with me toward the light all this while.

"No!" he said, pulling against me. "Something's in there!"

"It's just a bunch of trees. Come on!" I pulled forward and he pulled backward, but finally we got there.

The light was coming from inside a van. We walked closer. Aunt Amy's van! The driver's side door was hanging open, and the light from inside was what we had seen through the bushes. The van had crashed into the trees so that the passenger door was pinned shut.

We looked inside and there was her purse, sitting on the seat. We got in the van, closed the door so the light went off, and sat there close together without saying anything. That was a cold, lonely, dark place to be.

After a while Joaquin said, "I'm cold." I could feel his whole body shaking hard. We hadn't eaten anything since breakfast. Somehow we had to get warm enough to make our hands able to open our backpacks to get some food out. That meant we'd have to go inside a public building. We had a choice of a grocery store, a gas station, or the hospital. We talked about it, and I said that if we went to the hospital, maybe we could borrow some blankets to use in the van. We'd seen some lying around on empty beds. Joaquin agreed it was the best choice.

But we didn't know what a hospital expected from kids. There had been so few children in the hospital Momma stayed at with her pneumonia that we suspected kids might not be all that welcome. When we used to go visit Momma, the nurses always looked us up and down. Not one of them ever said, "And who's this Little Man?" to either one of us. That was a clear sign that either nurses were different kind of women or that the hospital was a different kind of place. Or both.

We waited out front until a family came along. Then we followed them in and found an empty room close to the outside stairwell where we could gather some blankets and pillows off beds that weren't being used. We sneaked out the back parking lot door and ran to Aunt Amy's van. It was still very cold and dark inside, but we locked the doors and curled up together with the blankets under and around us. Soon we were warm enough to rip open a package of peanuts. We fell asleep munching them.

In the middle of the night, Joaquin began to cry and it woke me up. He was very sad that Aunt Amy was lost. I was sad too. He asked me if I thought she had gone where Momma had gone. I didn't think so. I told him that as long as we hid in the van, nobody could take us away from Aunt Amy and that pretty soon she'd come back to get her car. It was about the only thing she owned, and I didn't think she'd go away and leave it on purpose.

Joaquin asked me if Momma would have gone away and left us if she'd had a car. I said it wasn't the same thing. He thought it was.

I said I figured Aunt Amy had to be in trouble or she wouldn't have left either us or her car. Joaquin said Momma hadn't been in trouble and she had left us.

I said Momma thought she was doing a good thing by leaving us with Aunt Amy, but that Aunt Amy thought it would be terrible to be without us. "She wouldn't leave on purpose, Joaquin. She has to be very, very sick."

Joaquin said, "So where is she?"

"Somewhere that makes sense . . . but I don't know where that is." I said that we just needed to be patient and keep a look out. Our job was to stay hidden, to stay with the van, and to keep searching the hospital.

Finally Joaquin stopped crying and said he agreed.

We were too hungry to go back to sleep, so I found one of our backpacks in the dark and felt around inside it until my fingers told me the shape was beef jerky and juice pouches. We chewed slowly until it became light outside and we could think about the real world instead of the night world of shadows and mystery sounds. Then we relaxed and fell asleep again.

## TWENTY-EIGHT

# GREY TOOTH

We woke up with the sound of glass crashing all around us. Our eyes opened into bright sunshine, which blinded us for a minute. Then we looked all around. The windows of the van weren't broken at all.

The sound of breaking glass came again. But this time we saw the ice come crashing down on the windshield. We both ducked. It was pretty funny and we started to laugh. The sun was melting the ice, which made some of it lose its grip and drop off the branches. The lightened load made the trees shiver, and then more ice would crack off. You'd be amazed how loud it was. Usually ice is a silent, gripping kind of thing. Not this ice. It was brilliant and shattered everywhere, falling through the air like crystal shards.

That first day we began what became our pattern: Once a day when we left the van, I locked it and put the key in my pocket and then we walked the rounds of the hospital floors. Another time, doing that could have made me feel grown up and important. As things were, it didn't: I felt too little for the job I had to do.

We made sure we went to the hospital at a different time each day so that people wouldn't get suspicious. We started to recognize people from one day to the next, but if they waved at one of us, we pretended not to notice. It wasn't a good thing to get too friendly. Joaquin wanted to visit with them. We were both getting lonely with just each other to talk to. I explained to him that we couldn't let people know anything about us or they'd ask us our names and where we lived and who we had come to see.

After a few days of searching, we knew that Aunt Amy wasn't in the hospital. Either that, or she was dead, and they were waiting for someone to come and get her so she could have a funeral and get buried. Every time that idea went through my mind, I'd get so sick to my stomach I'd want to double up and puke. But I couldn't say those things to Joaquin or he'd get the same way, and then where would we be?

We tried to imagine all sorts of places where they could have put her or taken her, and why. I was trying to decide how long we could last. Our backpacks were definitely lighter now, but it would be dangerous to start using the money in Aunt Amy's purse. I had no idea how much money we'd need to have when we found her, and there was nobody to tell our jokes to. Patients lying in hospital beds don't have wallets in their pockets.

We played around in the woods a little bit in the day-time, but we didn't dare show our faces in the stores or on the streets in case somebody recognized us from school. Joaquin thought we didn't have to worry because the school was on the other side of the town, but I was sure we did. I absolutely refused to go anywhere until it was starting to get late enough that kids had gone home, but not pitch dark so that we couldn't see to get back to the van.

We used our sight-dog skills for getting food without money. Hospitals have a lot of food that patients don't feel good enough to eat. We'd see it sitting on their plates on the kitchen stands in the halls when we'd be checking for Aunt Amy and it was the hardest thing in the world to walk off and leave it, especially knowing it was headed for the garbage can when we wished it was heading for our mouths.

At night just before everything in town closed up, we'd sometimes walk down the sidewalks smelling the hot suppers. That's when we discovered that another place for free food was the dumpster behind the grocery store. They would toss away packaged food when the date stamped on it was past. It was still safe to eat for a little while afterwards, though. My teacher had told us that companies did that to be on the safe side.

Joaquin and I had found a little plastic tub in the hospital dumpster that we were careful to fill with clean water from the service station bathroom for washing our food. The weather had turned warmer, so the dumpster food didn't freeze if you got to it before night time. Sometimes there would be sweet bananas with brown spots or other kinds of fruit that was just a little bit too soft.

The grocery store dumpster is where we met Grey Tooth

the first time. Joaquin was searching in the bin, and I was holding his legs so he wouldn't go in head first when Grey Tooth showed up. I pulled Joaquin down so we could make a run for it, but the man blocked our way, like he was going to beat us up. He walked up to Joaquin and said, "You, tough baby-man, you fight the wolf-man."

That made me mad. I'm the biggest. He should have picked on me, if he wasn't a chicken-heart himself. I told him to leave my little brother alone.

He bared his teeth and said, "I'm Grey Tooth, the lone wolf. Leave my dumpster alone. Get away from it!" He bared his grey teeth and growled at us and stuck his neck forward like he thought he could really be a fierce wolf.

I hadn't ever met anybody like him before, and he scared me plenty. I didn't think he was right in his head. I took Joaquin by the hand and we walked off without saying anything. I felt like my back side was exposed, like he could really get a few kicks in on us if he chose to. But I had the instinct that if we ran, he'd run after us. He wouldn't be able to resist two little kids running.

From then on, it was like everywhere we went we'd see Grey Tooth lurking somewhere. I truly hated it because I didn't know what he wanted from us. It was always like he was marking out territory. Any place that Joaquin and I went was already his territory. He probably wasn't any older than Cousin Bill and his friends, but his face had another look to it that was sort of old and mean. He breathed with his mouth open so his grey teeth always showed. I thought he called himself Grey Tooth because he thought a wolf name would help make him brave enough to survive.

One evening we were kicking rocks beside the emergency sign, trying to decide what to do for supper. We hadn't seen any sign of Grey Tooth yet that night and had already sneaked over to the grocery store dumpster. It was empty and so were our tummies. We kept on kicking rocks around, like it didn't matter that we were hungry. Pretty soon it was inky black outside and the cold was settling into the spaces around our necks and wrists where our coats were loose.

We noticed lights from a fast-food place farther on down the street so we trotted over and stopped by the window, listening to the hum of the neon tubes and smelling the food. I asked Joaquin if he thought we should spend some of our last money for a burger. He thought about it and said no. Then he pressed his face against the window to watch a high school boy we'd often seen working there do the closing-up jobs.

The high school worker saw Joaquin and his squashed nose on the glass and came to the door. He called to him, "Hey there, little Buddy."

Joaquin said, "You can't call me that."

I jabbed him with my elbow. Just because someone happens to guess a private thing of yours doesn't mean you have to admit it.

The hamburger worker said, "What?"

I said, "How's work tonight?" to give him something else to think about.

"Hey, if it isn't my friends, Buddy and Buster," he said.

That stopped me! Now I knew what it felt like to have

a dog's name. No wonder Joaquin had cried the first time I called him Buddy. I'd have to think about this.

The high school kid said, "It's closing time. I've got a couple of super-dupers I'm throwing out. Interested?"

We nodded our heads up and down. He filled two sacks with burgers and stuffed them to the brim with leftover fries. We both said, "Thanks a lot."

The food tasted wonderful. We ate it all up as we walked along in the night, before we ever got to the van. We locked the doors carefully and slept the whole night through without waking up once. That is a wonderful feeling.

When the morning light came in the van windows, I woke up thinking we were in our beds, safe and warm back in Aunt Amy's apartment, with school to go to in the morning after a big, hot breakfast.

Then I really woke up. None of that was true.

## TWENTY-NINE

# PAINFULLY BORED

Joaquin and I had a terrible lot of time with nothing much to do. It's hard to explain how very, very painful it is to be as bored as we were. I've tried to figure out why being bored hurts, but I've never been able to come up with any good answers. I simply know it does. Like the juicy places in your brain are dried up and creaking against each other. Chafing you bare and bleeding inside your mind.

We did all the same old things every day until even the dangerous ones, like playing in the woods during daylight started to get boring. The trees in the little wood weren't any good for climbing. The pine trees were too scratchy, and the branches weren't strong enough to hold us anyway. The other trees were the slim, bendable kind. None of them were sturdy enough to hold either of us off the ground so we could get a view of things. We had to leave the woods and our safe van to do that, and once we left the woods, I always felt like someone was going to discover us and take us away. Then how would we ever find Aunt Amy if we didn't wait for her where she said she'd be? I knew somewhere inside me that we had to wait. She'd come back for us if we could just figure out how to do the waiting long enough.

We were lucky it was a little town where the police or the mayor or whoever was in charge of keeping it tidy didn't notice that a crashed van called Old Noble Heart stayed parked a long time in the middle of a little woods. Most days we'd see police cars drive by the hospital and sometimes they'd wander through the parking lot, but they didn't ever stop at the woods. Maybe this town had a very busy mayor, or maybe one that didn't look around very much. This was a good thing for us. I'll bet all the vans that crash in bushes in Aunt Sandy's town get towed off pretty quick.

Joaquin said we should call Uncle Brett and tell him everything. I thought about it for a long time before I made an answer. I told him that if I could choose, I'd want Brady to be my brother and Uncle Brett to be my dad. But Uncle Brett had a great big family already. That's why they had to have a nanny. If we asked to live with them, maybe they'd have to have two nannies, which would take a lot of money. I didn't want to tell Joaquin what the biggest reason was because it would hurt his feelings. But finally I had to.

At the family council when Uncle Marc had said that Aunt Amy wasn't doing a good job and couldn't keep us anymore, Uncle Brett had not said, "I want the boys." He hadn't said anything at all. If he had wanted us, he would have said, "Let us take the boys." He didn't. But Aunt Amy really wanted us. She wanted us so bad she cried her eyes out over maybe losing us. That's who needed us. That's who we had to find.

Joaquin wasn't convinced. He said maybe Uncle Brett would want us if he thought about it a little while.

I said, "Aunt Amy is who really wants us. We've got to find her, Joaquin."

One day when I was pretending to drive the van, I turned the key in the motor to see if it would start. It made a grinding sound, but the motor didn't go. Maybe the battery was used up from having the light on so long the day Aunt Amy crashed into the woods. So now we knew Old Noble Heart had turned into Scuffy.

We were glad to have the Chinese checkers game and played that every day. Six people can play, so we used my backpack for Brady, Joaquin's backpack for Carmen, Aunt Amy's purse for her, and the checkers box for somebody else, like Collette. We switched everybody around so that everybody played all of the colors. Sometimes we'd make one person play stupid and lose.

My card games passed the time for us too. We learned all the games in the instruction book and then we made a kind of combination card game and Chinese checkers. It was pretty complicated and we'd make up different rules every day that we couldn't ever remember for even the whole game. We could have quarreled over it, I suppose, but we'd just fall over laughing and call each other stupid names.

The weather became quite a bit warmer, so sleeping in the van became more comfortable. We used the woods to pee in, which neither of us enjoyed. It wasn't fun like during the summer with Brady. At some point in the day, however, we always had to find a real restroom. The ground was too frozen to dig, and besides, we didn't have any toilet paper in our backpacks. Sometimes we'd use the hospital or the grocery store restrooms, but the closest and best place was the gas station.

But there were two problems there. One: we were scared they'd see too much of us and get suspicious as to why we were always coming around and didn't buy any gas. Two: Grey Tooth had marked it as his territory. There were enough people around that I didn't think he'd dare hurt us there, but every single time we went there, he was always lurking around. He'd come over kind of close and snarl at us. He didn't threaten to fight us again because he knew we wouldn't. But I always worried that he'd follow us back to the van. He had to know where we slept. He was weird, but he wasn't totally stupid.

Even though the weather started to get warmer, it hadn't been warm long enough to dry out the grass. Our feet got wet and stayed that way, which was very cold and uncomfortable. I looked at Joaquin and saw how muddy and dirty he was. That meant I was too. I knew we needed baths just awful. The only good thing about being that dirty was that maybe it would keep people from school from recognizing us. But unless you've been really dirty for a long time, you might not think about how itchy it gets.

We began concentrating on how to get a bath and sometimes at night we'd walk around, trying to figure out how to do it. We walked past the town swimming pool, but the sign said it was closed until the end of May. We thought of sneaking into the town motel and taking a shower and then leaving, but that was pretty desperate and scary. Besides, we could never find any doors that were open. We watched cars going through the car wash and considered that possibility for a while. Then one night we tried it.

The car wash was going to close soon and no cars were inside. We walked up and put some coins into the slot like we'd seen the grown-ups do and then turned on the sprayer. The water was warm, but it came at us so hard that it kind of hurt, even when we stood on the far side of the cement stall with our clothes on and our backs to the spray. We came out a lot cleaner than we went in, though, and that was a good thing.

The next problem was that the blast of air that dries off a car isn't nearly enough to dry off wet clothes. We ran back to the van in the cold night air and by the time we got to the van, we were shivering so hard we could hardly untie our shoes. We struggled to get out of our wet clothes and hung them over bushes. Then we scrambled into the van, locked the doors as usual, and slept naked in our blankets through the night. For sure it felt way better than sleeping in our crusty old jeans and T-shirts.

During the night it rained and the next morning we stared out the windows at where the wind had blown our clothes into the mud. We knew how to work the machines at the laundromat, of course, but we had to figure out what to wear while we got them clean.

I could wash Joaquin's clothes while he stayed in the

blankets in the van, but there was no way I was going to let him go by himself to wash my clothes. I said he had to stay locked inside the van while I was gone and not to even stick his nose out the window until I got back.

It was a lucky thing I said that too because who should come lurking around the laundromat but Grey Tooth. He was pretending to be a wolf as usual. When I'd see him peering around the corner outside the window, he'd crouch down behind a car, hiding. He could have come into the laundromat after me, but he never did. Sometimes there were people coming and going, but I was often alone for a little while.

I thought quite a bit about him while I was watching the clothes tumble dry. What had he been like when he was my age? Did he have a family somewhere? Why didn't he live with them? Why was he all alone? Why didn't he get a job? What went wrong in his brain? I had to make up the answers, which amounted to me telling myself a story.

But the real story underneath that one was a story that worried me. What would happen to me and to Joaquin over time, if Aunt Amy didn't come back? How long could we go on living like this while we waited for her? If I never lived in a house or went to school again, would I become like Grey Tooth? No education, dirty clothes, stealing food from dumpsters, pretending to be a wolf?

# THIRTY

# ALIEN WOMAN

There was nothing to mark one day as different from
another, really. What worried me was that we might
get careless and miss something important going on in the
hospital. We still searched each floor daily and sometimes,
when there were new people in the beds, we'd try to look
them over a little more carefully than the rest. We'd been
watching the patients long enough that we pretty much
knew who was who by the shapes in the bed.

We'd seen bloody bandages and legs in white casts,
strung up in the air. We'd heard people crying out for help.
But none of our searching prepared us for what we'd find
when we actually found Aunt Amy.

First off, we only half recognized her. We saw that a new
woman was in one of the beds that had been empty (the
hospital put more blankets in the room). She had a white
bandage around her head that had a little oozy blood under
one section. Her face was gross—swollen completely out of

shape. One eye was bulgy and drooping, even when shut. She had tubes going in her veins and she was hooked up to machines that monitored just about everything on her body.

We both stared for awhile, but the woman had her eyes closed and didn't notice us standing there. Then we said her name to make sure it really was her, but the woman in the bed didn't even flinch. Didn't respond in any way. I crept a little closer to read the name on her wrist band. It was a number.

I told Joaquin we'd made a mistake. It wasn't Aunt Amy.

Joaquin said it was her.

I said it wasn't.

We agreed to look for some other clues in case it really was Aunt Amy and somebody was playing a bad trick on us. We started to go through the cupboards in her room, looking for something to give us a hint about this woman that mostly didn't look like Aunt Amy but kind of reminded you of a person you used to know. We heard people coming down the hall, so Joaquin and I stepped inside a little storage closet where we'd been looking for clues.

The nurse with short black hair said in a surprised voice, "She's back!"

The short, soft nurse said, "General sent her back to us in case her family comes looking for her here."

"Hey, I heard about how she came dragging into Emergency on her hands and knees, mud everywhere. Poor thing."

"Amazing she made it. Aneurysm."

"Totally amazing. Anterior descending artery with clips front and back. I saw the CT-scans. Not many make a full recovery."

"She's got a long road ahead of her."

They tried to make conversation with the woman in the bed, but she didn't answer them.

When the nurses left, we tiptoed out of the closet and looked at the freaky alien woman lying in the bed. Joaquin called softly, "Aunt Amy."

Nothing.

I looked carefully at the face in the bed over and over again. If it really was Aunt Amy, maybe some aliens had gotten to her. Maybe the aliens had made her forget how to talk. That could have happened. I saw it on a TV show once.

We slept in the van, same as usual, but we woke up early in the morning and ran to the alien woman's room. Two storage cupboards in her room were very large, so we each crawled inside one of them to wait. That was better than standing still in the tall closet like yesterday. I left the door of my cupboard open a crack.

A doctor come by before breakfast and tried to talk to the woman in the bed. He took her hand and squeezed it a little, but she wouldn't open her eyes. She didn't even move her eyes underneath their eyelids to show she had heard him. A little later a nurse came by to wash her face and hands and feet. I thought the nurse could have done a better job. She didn't even smooth lotion on her skin afterward.

Breakfast came on a tray, but the woman didn't wake up

then either. Joaquin whispered that he was hungry and if she didn't want to eat, he sure did. Then we heard a nurse tell another one to make sure they kept a record of how much she ate and drank. I thought that would be a simple job since we could plainly see she wasn't eating or drinking anything. But we couldn't steal her food. It would make the numbers turn out wrong.

We watched the plates of food the patients didn't eat being taken out to big racks in the hall. Food that was going to be thrown away. We were very hungry, our backpacks were nearly flat, and it was hard to watch. Joaquin said it wouldn't matter if we took food after they had already written down what the patients had eaten. I knew we'd get caught and told him not to. But Joaquin said he had his own thinks about it.

Now that we had quit school I believed it was my responsibility to make sure Joaquin knew the correct way to speak, even though he didn't go to first grade any more. "The word should be 'thoughts,' " I said.

"I have my own thinks," he repeated. Sometimes he's stubborn.

"No. It's supposed to be, 'I have my own thoughts.' "

"Uncle Brett thinks this, the doctor thinks that, and I think something else. We all have our own thinks."

I didn't say anything more about it. He was being a stubborn little Buddy.

Then, without even telling me, he darted out into the hall and grabbed two apples and two bags of chips off the carts. We ate in the cupboards and watched the alien woman, lying still in her bed. By the time it was dark, our legs were cramped, so we decided to go out to the van. The people from the kitchen must have forgotten the carts on that floor of the hospital because the leftover food was still standing there on the trays. On our way toward the back steps, Joaquin and I filled our pockets with rolls and pudding cups and bags of carrots, anything that was dry or in a package we could carry. We ate every bit of it that night in the van; we ate until our tummies were round.

The next morning we got up really early so that we were tucked into the hospital cupboards when the doctors came. The tall doctor said she was lucky to be alive. I looked at her totally gross, unconscious face and wasn't sure she'd feel that way if she ever woke up.

The other one said that she wasn't progressing as well as they had hoped. "Have any family come forward?"

The nurses told him no.

"That's too bad. Sometimes family members can help in ways the rest of us can't. It's like they give them hope, so the patient tries a little harder."

"The police were in and took fingerprints."

"Results?"

"No. They didn't connect with anything."

"Not good. She needs family." He shook his head and paused in the doorway. I hoped maybe he'd say more about the fingerprinting. I was very sorry we'd missed out on that. But he just sighed and walked out.

While the hospital was still full of visitors and nobody would notice a couple extra, Joaquin and I started pulling out all the drawers in the alien woman's room. We had to know for sure if it was Aunt Amy or not. Joaquin was trying to talk to her, whispering her name. I crept up softly and opened the big door underneath her night table. Bingo! A large plastic bag. I pulled it out. Full of clothes. Aunt Amy's clothes. Very muddy clothes.

"Let's go," I said to Joaquin. We had our answer.

That night as we were falling asleep in the van I thought about aliens and Dead Uncle Dick. I had only half believed in ghosts and aliens before, but seeing Aunt Amy this way was starting to change my mind.

# THIRTY-ONE
# GOOD-BYE SCUFFY

In the morning, Joaquin and I started on a new plan. It had happened in my brain during the night when I didn't even know a plan was going on in my head. I woke up with it. I told him we needed to show up in the hospital as Aunt Amy's family. If we talked to her all day long, maybe that would help her want to start talking again.

It felt strange walking into the hospital like we belonged there. When the nurses came in to check on Aunt Amy, we told them we were there to help our Aunt Amy get better. You should have seen the surprised looks on their faces. They started asking our names and addresses. We gave them our names all right, but I told them the old address where we used to live. We did not tell them about any of the uncles. I said our car broke down in town as we were driving through on our vacation. Joaquin glared at me because he hates lies.

When the nurse with the black hair walked out, I heard

her say, "You know, I've seen these little guys wandering around the hospital before. I just didn't connect them with our patient."

Every morning we'd take a good look at the person in the bed and she was always just enough like Aunt Amy to make us feel homesick for her. We'd stroke her cheeks and squeeze her hands. I sang her every song I ever learned from the movie DVDs.

Nothing happened.

One day we took a break from the hospital to wash Aunt Amy's muddy clothes along with our own at the laundromat. I hadn't seen Grey Tooth for a few days, and that was good news. We folded Aunt Amy's clean clothes into the plastic bag and put it back where we had found it in her night stand.

We were planning on having some lunch in the back of the van, but when we entered the little forest, we were very surprised to see a bright yellow band around the van's windshield. I knew what it meant. The police had found us. They thought it was just an abandoned van, crashed in the woods. They didn't know it held precious things, like the rest of our food hoard and Aunt Amy's purse. They didn't know it was Aunt Amy's only possession and that she was coming back for it.

Joaquin asked if I knew what the yellow band meant.

I said, "Yes. Pretty soon the police are going to tow the van away."

"What are we going to do?" he asked me.

"We are going to wake Aunt Amy up."

That afternoon I carried Aunt Amy's purse into the hospital and put it on top of her clothes under the night stand. We put our backpacks that were almost flat now into the storage cupboards. I felt urgent about everything and kind of angry that Aunt Amy wouldn't even try. We'd waited for her to come back. We'd taken care of the van as long as we could. How could we make her know we were there? How could we make her try a little harder for us?

Joaquin and I each took one of her hands and rubbed them gently, over and over again, while we stared hard at her ugly alien face. After a few minutes of that I said, "Hello, Aunt Amy," medium-loud, same as usual.

Never once had she said anything back. But this time her bulgy eye flickered and she said, "Hi."

I nearly jumped out of my own skin.

One side of her face was sagging, but she could lift the other side a little to smile. She said, "Hi, you guys."

I almost cried I was so happy. I said, "I'm glad you're awake now."

Joaquin was kind of jigging up and down. "You were asleep a long time, Aunt Amy."

Aunt Amy said, "Long time."

"Where did they take you, Aunt Amy?" Joaquin wanted to know.

She said, "They left me here."

"Who?"

"They did."

"Who did?" Joaquin asked.

"Those people," she said.

"Who do you mean, Aunt Amy?" I asked.

She waved her hand around in the air a little and said, "Don't take water away."

Joaquin was confused. "You don't have any water."

She said, "Want water," very loudly in a croaky voice.

The nurse heard her and walked into the room with this totally surprised face. "So what have we here?"

Aunt Amy said, "Water."

The nurse smiled and patted her hand and said, "You're making wonderful progress. I'll get you some water."

Aunt Amy called after her, "Squirts! Water."

The nurse returned with a glass of water and helped Aunt Amy suck it up through a straw. After a few sips, the nurse said, "I see your family is here to see you."

Aunt Amy said, "Water."

The nurse helped her drink one more time and then asked, "So, how are you doing?"

Aunt Amy's one opened eye rolled around the room a little and then she said, "Pickles. In the drawer. Pickles."

The nurse opened the bedside table drawer to look and said, "No, there's no pickles in here. Now, you just get some more rest."

Aunt Amy promptly closed her good eye and I believe went to sleep.

Back in the van that night Joaquin whispered to me, "Aunt Amy doesn't make sense."

"I know," I whispered back. And that was about the state of things.

Every day after that we'd try to visit with Aunt Amy—

just a little time here and there, but we'd come back all day long. No matter how the conversation started, after a few sentences Aunt Amy would lose track of her ideas. She had lots of ideas, but they didn't fit into proper spaces anymore. Joaquin seemed as puzzled by her as I was. We didn't understand why she couldn't think very well anymore. If we didn't take care of her, would she end up like Grey Tooth, out on the streets digging through dumpsters? I hadn't even finished fifth grade yet, and I knew for a fact how little money there was left in Aunt Amy's wallet. How could I do it all?

First things first. I had to get Aunt Amy out of the hospital and home. She had to convince the hospital people she was well enough to leave. And it had to be soon, because the van had been wearing the yellow band for five days already.

That evening the bushes had a little hint of green on the stems, which was just enough life to wish on. I wished that we could wander into these woods near the hospital and come out another side of the woods into a world where Aunt Amy was strong and made sense. I wished it again and again, but when I opened my eyes the last time, none of it was real.

Finally I fell asleep in the locked van, the hunger and the cold lurking around the edges of the hospital blankets. The moon was bright that night and shone through the windows. Joaquin fell asleep immediately like he usually did, but my mind wouldn't quiet down. I had to figure out how Aunt Amy was thinking to know where her mind got off track. The town dogs were barking something fierce, which bothered me, but finally I drifted off.

In the middle of the night I woke up, startled. I lay still

as can be to hear again what my unconscious mind had heard in my sleep. Nothing. Joaquin was breathing deeply. There was no wind. The sounds of silence filled the van. I began to drift off into a light sleep again. The dogs from town were once again baying at the full moon when I woke up startled a second time.

Something was wrong. But I didn't know what. It just felt dark and empty all around me. Then I heard it. Scratching at the door. A light tapping on the glass. I opened my eyes. There, framed in the moonlight, was the face of Grey Tooth, staring at me through the window.

I pretended I hadn't seen him and closed my eyes except for little slits so that I could detect movement. I needed to know if he had moved off or if he would try to enter the van somehow. He stayed there, staring at us as we slept inside the van. I knew then what Grey Tooth wanted: our van. He wanted it for himself. That's what he wanted from us and had wanted all along.

Then the face left the window, and I heard him howl in the middle of the little forest—howl, like he really was a wolf. And I felt so sorry for a man, a boy who should be in high school, who had the idea that it would be better to be a wolf than a boy. So very sad. I didn't go back to sleep.

When Joaquin woke up from the sunshine in the windows, I announced we had just spent our last night sleeping in the van. We folded up the blankets and pillows, carried them back into the hospital, and stowed them in the cupboards in Aunt Amy's room. No way would I ever again sleep in the van in the woods with Grey Tooth prowling.

After Aunt Amy finished her breakfast, I took the food tray out to the hall, wiped her face and hands and the table with a wash cloth, and dried her off with a towel. (Aunt Amy was a very messy eater these days and spilled food everywhere.) Then I rubbed hospital lotion all over her hands and arms and cheeks. She laid her head back on the pillow and closed her eyes for a few minutes and I let her. After just a little while had gone by, though, I lifted out her purse and set it on the hospital tray, which I pulled across her bed. Joaquin and I both quietly called her name a few times until she opened her eyes. Her eyes went straight forward to where her purse was sitting on the tray and she made a kind of gurgle in her throat. She recognized it.

While she watched, I took out her wallet and removed her driver's license, along with a couple of other kinds of important looking cards and laid them out, all in a row, on the tray table. I told Aunt Amy that we wanted to take her back to the summer cottage at the lake. She had to tell the hospital people who she was; she needed to pay them for their care of her. We had to do it today. I would get a taxi to take us home. I told her what to say in simple words over and over.

When the nurses came in the next time, you should have seen their faces. Aunt Amy said, "Go home today. Get me papers. Sign papers." Joaquin and I were standing with our backs to the window watching it all, but not saying anything.

Did those nurses ever scurry! They had the hospital registration people up to the room so fast you wouldn't believe it. They filled out all the forms using the cards I had laid out. Aunt Amy signed her name. It was the sloppiest signature I'd ever seen. It didn't look even a little bit like the signature on her driver's license. But then, her alien face didn't look much like the picture on the driver's license either.

When the doctors came in that morning, Aunt Amy was dressed in her clean clothes and sitting in a chair with her purse on her lap. The nurses thought Aunt Amy had dressed herself, but that's not how it happened. They left to do some errands and while they were gone, Joaquin and I dressed Aunt Amy, brushed her hair, and buckled her shoes. She did everything we told her to do. Stand up. Sit down. Stick out your foot. Turn around. She didn't say one word. I looked at her face after we got her ready and I could tell she was tired. I told her she couldn't sleep until we were in the taxi.

She said, "Okay."

When the doctors came in, they were surprised to see her dressed and sitting there. The tallest one said, "And how are we doing today, Amy?"

She said, "I'm going home today."

He wasn't sure what to say and just stared at her for a few moments.

I supplemented, "We have a taxi coming right away."

The doctor said okay, and started working on the papers that said she could leave the hospital. Joaquin and I heard some engine noises outside the window and turned around to look at what was going on. There was a police car beside the little woods. A tow truck had Aunt Amy's van hooked up and it was dragging Scuffy out of the woods. Grey Tooth was watching. I know the police and the tow truck man couldn't see him from where they were standing because he was crouched behind a very dense prickle bush, peeping out from time to time. Joaquin and I watched Old Noble Heart as it was pulled off down the road, and we wanted to wave good-bye.

Grey Tooth watched it go too and started to trot down the street after it. I imagine him, now, living in the town junk yard and forgetting to close Scuffy's doors. That's a sad end for Aunt Amy's van, but maybe Grey Tooth is happy to have a home.

The taxi driver was pleased about the big fare we were going to give him when we got to the summer cottage and was very helpful about getting Aunt Amy settled in the back seat with the seat belt on. She didn't say one word on the drive, and soon closed her eyes, her head falling forward. The morning had completely exhausted her.

I sat up front with the driver to give directions on how to take us to the summer cottage. As we entered the lake area, we saw a "For Sale" sign on the lawn in front of the lake house. If Joaquin and I had seen it go up before Aunt Amy went to the hospital, we'd have probably cried our eyes out for days. But after what we had been through, it didn't matter so much. I simply told the taxi driver to turn to the right.

We were as careful as we could be about waking Aunt Amy and helping her out of the taxi. I lifted one of her feet out onto the ground and then the other and then put both my arms around her waist to steady her. She stood there, still as she could be, smelling the fresh air, while Joaquin lifted our empty backpacks out of the taxi.

When Joaquin handed the driver the money, he said it was further than he'd figured and we had to pay him three of the twenty-dollar bills instead of two. Joaquin had no choice but to give them to him, even though it wasn't fair to change the price.

Inside, everything was exactly the same as when we left after the ice storm: the dirty dishes sitting in the sink and the mussy beds. Plus a fresh crop of spiderwebs. Yuck.

## THIRTY-TWO

# RIGHT NOW

So now you know how Joaquin and Aunt Amy and I got here and why we're in such a tough spot. The muddy walk I told you about to begin with probably makes a whole lot more sense to you now.

And you can probably also tell that I haven't got a single plan for getting us out of our troubles. They're still all the same old ones: we're running low on food and we're almost out of money. For as long as I've been working on these two problems, you'd think I'd have them figured out. And on top of that, we're running low on fuel for the generator. If the generator stops, nights will be cold and dark. I don't think Aunt Amy could live through that.

Joaquin went searching in the little shed beside the summer cottage while I tended Aunt Amy. He came back dragging an old red wagon with high wooden sides. It looks like I'll have to walk into town and buy another tank of fuel and a few more groceries. Nobody is out here at the lake yet, so I'll be walking the whole twenty miles there and another twenty miles back. I wonder how many days that will take me.

I'm scared to leave Joaquin with Aunt Amy. He's only six years old. But he's good and brave and very smart. I hope they don't run out of the canned food while I'm gone because Joaquin isn't quite as good at making pancakes as I am.

Aunt Amy used to be good and brave and smart too. Now she's . . . well, there's no use saying it.

# THIRTY-THREE

# NEW OWNERS

I had a little bit of luck on the way into town. The electric company had come out to check on some houses, so the worker guys gave me a ride into town. They said that now spring was here, people were going to be coming back to the houses around the lake any day. The guys were cheery and didn't ask nosy questions. When I grow up, that's the kind of adult I plan to be.

While I was at the grocery store, I saw a rack of garden seeds and decided that was the answer to one of our biggest problems. If Joaquin and I plant a garden, we'll have food for the whole summer. It was fun picking out the seed packets. I got the vegetables we like best: peas, carrots, lettuce, tomatoes, and corn. I don't know too much about how squash tastes, but the flowers in the picture were so beautiful that I had to buy a package of that too.

Best of all, I found a package with a picture of a beautiful green mint plant on the outside, so Aunt Amy can have some fresh mint tea. That should perk her up.

I was lucky again on the trip home. I was pulling my wagon full of groceries and the tank of generator fuel onto the dirt road that leads twenty miles down to the lake. It was very heavy and slow going, so I knew I'd have to spend the night sleeping in a field. Then a man and a woman drove up beside me in their car and stopped to ask me if I needed help or a ride somewhere.

They had really nice faces that showed what they were like inside, so I said I was going clear down to the lake. How far were they going?

They were going to the lake too.

I said I didn't know where we'd put the wagon.

They said to wait a minute. Their moving truck would be along right away and we could put the wagon in the front seat beside the driver.

I said the driver wasn't going to like that.

They laughed and said he wouldn't care. Besides, it wasn't far to the lake.

They wanted to visit and find out all about me, but I didn't dare do that. I did my best to be very nice and polite and not say much, because I wasn't even sure what name to give them. I thought telling my real name was a stupid choice, of course, even though they didn't look like laughers. I wasn't comfortable about saying I was Brady Walker, either. And there was less truth now about the initials name (LKC) than ever before. Without some kind of plan, silence was my only choice.

Pretty soon they got the hint and stopped asking me

questions. We sat in the car together without talking, but it wasn't a grumpy or irritated silence. It was just a quiet time until the truck came along.

As things turned out, they were the people who had bought our family lake house because the truck pulled in the driveway. I said I'd get my wagon out and pull it the rest of the way home. They tried to insist that I put it in their trunk with the lid up so they could drive me home, but I said I could do it myself. I headed out into the woods and made a big circle around the lake so they couldn't tell where I lived.

When I told Joaquin about them, we both got really excited. Maybe they would need jobs done and we could earn some money. The shopping trip had left us with four dollars and sixty-two cents. You could say we're about broke.

I am trying to like the new owners as much as I did at first, now that I know they get to live in our family's beautiful home. I feel jealous when I think about them inside the lake house. I guess I've got to start seeing it another way if I'm ever going to be happy again.

Another thing, how can I learn a new way to think about Aunt Amy? There's no way to be happy about how she is now. None. She says weird things, can't dress herself without falling over, and is always trying to run away from us.

Joaquin was the first to get a job with Richard and Charlotte, the new people in our lake house. He was so curious about them that he had to go peeking around their place until they discovered him. He told them he was my brother and they said we could both do jobs for them if we wanted to. Of course we did, but we said only one of us could work at a time since we had responsibilities at home. We didn't explain that meant someone had to stay home and tend Aunt Amy.

She is very regular in her habits. If we feed her at the same time every day, then we know exactly when she'll take naps and go to bed and get up. But one of us always has to be with her in the house. She can't be alone one single minute. She gets scared over the littlest things and cries because she can't do stuff. That means that Joaquin is going to be working alone with the new neighbors. I'm not worried they'll turn out to be mean people or anything, but I've already said how Joaquin is about telling all the truth about himself. He can't help it. It just spills out all over him.

I warn him absolutely every time he leaves the house that he isn't allowed to tell them any name except HM. None of the other names are true anymore anyway. And he can only think about being a sight dog, looking for food, money, and information.

Joaquin says real sight dogs only have one thing to concentrate on, not three. This is true. The first time he said this, I asked him what he thought the one thing should be for him. He said he might change it every day, but he'd like to start out looking for information. I agreed. Richard and Charlotte are planting a garden and we need to learn how so we can plant ours.

THIRTY-FOUR

# PAYING JOBS

Before I tell you what we're doing now, you need to understand how lonely we were. For weeks we hid in the van or the hospital and hardly spoke to another person besides each other. We like each other a lot and never fight—I already explained about kids who waste themselves on stupid stuff—but we were tired of each other's ideas. We needed more ideas in our heads, new ideas.

Working in the garden was perfect for new ideas. We learned how to dig the soil and pull out the roots; how to rake it smooth; how to make a little ditch for the seeds in a straight line by tying a string to two little posts; how deep to place the seeds and how to space them out according to instructions on the back of the packets; and finally, how to cover the seeds up and tamp the soil down gently. Joaquin and I worked hard to do the same thing in our garden as we had done in Richard and Charlotte's. Our garden didn't turn out to have smooth dark soil like theirs. On this side of the lake there are more rocks, and the soil is grey. People haven't dug up the garden at the summer cottage very much, so the dead weeds lying on it were very thick and heavy to haul away.

Richard and Charlotte warned us that the hardest part was when you had to water and weed. But that won't be for a month or so. I honestly don't know if we can wait a month for our garden to grow food. We don't have that many cans or packets left in the cupboard. I've told Joaquin that he needs to change his sight-dog approach to focus on money. I'm going to keep mine on food. Together we'll think up a plan. We have to.

Richard and Charlotte pay us every day. Often they invite us to stay for supper with them afterward, which is going to stretch out our food a little more than eleven days. I watch how they work together in the kitchen, and it looks like they know where the other one is going to move next. Like they're doing a little dance. Sometimes I relax and smile while I watch them. Joaquin says he does too.

I told them we had a big dog at home that liked table scraps. After that they took to heaping up a big plate for one boy to carry back home. More food than just one brother could possibly eat.

Aunt Amy likes their cooking very much and is starting to gain back some of the weight she lost in the hospital. Her eyes aren't as bulgy now and her cheek bones don't stick out quite as much. She's still not as pretty as before, though. Her hair is straggly and getting very long. She won't let Joaquin or me brush it because she says we hurt her. She does it herself and she does a very sloppy job.

After that muddy walk I told you about, when she became too tired, we haven't let her outside. Now that people are starting to move into the houses on the other side of the lake, we don't dare let her go outside in case she'll make a fuss. Every minute she's awake we're afraid she'll escape. There's nothing much Joaquin and I could do to stop her from doing anything she wanted to, if she put her mind to it. But she still doesn't concentrate very well, which helps us.

She hasn't called us by our names since she came home, but I'm pretty sure she knows exactly who we are. We only use initials now. Joaquin is HM and I'm SM. Hungry Man and Stick Man. What a pair.

Our problem is not knowing exactly who Aunt Amy is anymore. It might be that her mind is giving her good ideas but that her mouth has lost the words. Sort of like when my tongue didn't make words well until I taught it what to do by chewing and chewing and chewing. It's hard to tell what's going on inside Aunt Amy's mind.

Joaquin and I take shifts with Aunt Amy. He'll go work with Richard and Charlotte for an hour and then I'll go work with them for an hour. We keep on doing that for as long as they need us. We don't have watches so we ask them to tell us the time.

Yesterday Joaquin didn't come back when he was supposed to. It was getting dark and still no Joaquin. Since he hadn't come back with a plate of supper for us, I made pancakes and put Aunt Amy to bed. When she was asleep, I went out to look for him. He was sitting on the private path we'd made through the woods from the lake house to the summer cottage. Sitting there, crying his eyes out.

I thought maybe he'd fallen down and was hurt. He said he wasn't hurt except for in his chest. He looked all right to me, so I asked him what had happened that was so bad. He said that he had been very happy that day. The happiest day since the cousins had come at Christmas time. Charlotte and Richard had given him apple slices and a peanut butter sandwich before he started the new job of stacking wood neatly in a pile. (The garden work is finished for a little while.) Richard said Joaquin sure was a good worker. The food and the compliment made him forget about secrets.

He started to tell about playing in the lake house—where they live now—all last summer while it was still the family's and being scared of Dead Uncle Dick, who was a ghost coming back, and all the fun with cousins named Carmen and Brady and how Momma had gotten pneumonia after the butterfly of true love left her shoulder and then she went away for always and how Aunt Amy had taught us how to cook but now that she was out of the hospital she said silly things all day and we only had seven cans and three packets left in the cupboard.

All of a sudden he realized what he was saying and took a look at Richard's and Charlotte's faces. When he saw how they were looking at him, he took off running. He whizzed past a couple of houses and then ducked up the hill so they couldn't see where he entered our hidden path. He felt so terrible about giving away most of our secrets that he knew he couldn't ever come back and tell me. So that was why he was sitting on the path, crying. He had nowhere safe to go.

I felt a lot of things. Mad like I wanted to punch him. Sad for his crying like I wanted to hug him. Scared like I wanted to take his hand and start running far away, running forever and ever. I just stood there like I was frozen.

After a few minutes he wiped off some tears and asked me what we were going to do. I squatted down beside him and put my arm around his bony shoulders. "We're going back to Aunt Amy before she busts out of there. And we're going to grow things in our own garden. And we're never going to work for Richard and Charlotte or see them again."

Joaquin sniffed all the way home and wiped his nose on his shirt, but he said I had a good plan.

## THIRTY-FIVE

# SHE ESCAPES

The plan didn't even work for one day. When I got Joaquin home, I went to the cupboard to count the cans left. There weren't any, just a little pancake flour for breakfast. But, we have almost twenty-eight dollars between us from working, plus a few dollars left from Aunt Amy's purse, so I planned to set out for town with the wagon as soon as it was light.

Very early some men started banging on our roof. One was pulling out the limbs from the ice storm that were stabbing through the ceiling. Another man was ripping off the ruined shingles. Both were throwing things around and making a huge mess all over the yard. I hoped they wouldn't walk on our new garden.

When I looked out the window to see who was making the racket, I saw Richard's face. I ducked down so that he didn't see me. Why would he be coming around the summer cottage acting like he was in charge? It made me very angry.

He'd already gotten our lake home, but he had no right coming over here to this one.

Then about the worst thing in the world happened. Aunt Amy took a look out the bedroom window on her side of the room where it was lower down. She saw Richard and Charlotte, and it was like she went berserk. She thrashed around with her nightgown on so bad that it took both Joaquin and me to get it off her and pull on her blouse and skirt. Then she started hauling on the door handle yelling, "Out! Out! Out!"

Maybe if Joaquin and I had had breakfast we'd have been a little stronger, but after a few minutes, Richard and Charlotte started to knock on the other side of the door. Joaquin and I knew it was all over, so we let go of Aunt Amy's arms and dived under the beds. She would have to enter the world as she was, but it didn't mean we had to. At least not yet.

I expected Richard and Charlotte would get tired of her company right away and send her back in the house. Then we'd slide out quickly from under the beds and lock her in. After, when all the men went to lunch, I'd sneak up the hill with my wagon and get on the road to town a ways above where the road for the other lake houses joined the main road so Richard and Charlotte would never see me.

It didn't happen like that.

Things stayed quiet for a while and Aunt Amy did not come back inside. I wondered if Richard and Charlotte didn't realize Aunt Amy was not a person who could take care of herself. Maybe they had let her wander around on her own.

If so, I'd have to go chase her down after the workmen on the roof went home. She could be a long ways off by then.

Finally I got too tense to lie under the bed and think about the possibilities. I crawled out and pulled myself up to look out the window. I half expected to see Aunt Amy busting down the path around the lake, holding out her skirts and swinging them from left to right like she did the few times we took her outside for a walk.

That's not at all what she was doing. What I saw was a sight I couldn't have guessed in a million years of guessing. She was standing very still and Richard had both his arms around her, holding her tight.

After I closed my mouth from that surprise, I saw him let go of her and Charlotte did the same thing. Then Richard wrapped his arms around them both and they all three stood that way for so long I started to fidget.

I was thinking it might be a good break for Joaquin if I took him to town with me. If we left Aunt Amy with Richard and Charlotte for the day, since they seemed to think so much of her company, it wouldn't be any harder to hunt for her when she escaped from them as it would when she escaped from Joaquin. I knew he'd never be able to keep her inside now. Besides, it might be nice to share Aunt Amy with somebody else for a while.

But that's not how it happened either.

## THIRTY-SIX

# FAMILY GHOST

Richard and Charlotte knocked on the door. I whispered to Joaquin to stay hidden under the bed no matter what happened. Then they all came in. I could see their feet: Richard had on big brown work shoes, Charlotte wore yellow rubber boots with white flowers and green leaves, and Aunt Amy's feet were bare and all red up to the ankles. They looked cold enough to hurt really bad.

Then the absolutely worst thing happened. Richard and Charlotte called both our real names: Cheyenne, Joaquin. I was scared. How did they know? Had Aunt Amy remembered our names and told on us?

Richard's shoes walked into the bedroom, and I braced myself against the wall under the headboard. He knelt down between the beds and lifted up the skirts of one bed and then the other with his long arms. He could see exactly where we were and tried to coax us out. I could see Joaquin was slammed up against the wall just like me. Neither one of us were planning to come out without the best struggle we had.

Then he did a surprising thing. He sat down on the floor and laughed. It was one of those laughs where a person's whole body shakes because he's loose and happy. That made me curious enough to start looking for what he would do next.

But I never expected what he'd say. "Boys, I'm Dead Uncle Dick." And he kept on laughing.

Joaquin said, "No, you're not."

Richard said, "Yes, I am."

Joaquin said. "No, you're not. Dead Uncle Dick is a ghost."

Aunt Amy got tired of watching. Her red feet walked away and Charlotte's boots clumped after her. Richard still sat on the floor between the beds. I knew his butt would get sore before mine would. Unless spiders started coming out to look me over. I hate spiders.

Richard said, "I'm your uncle Richard. I'm less dead than I ever have been before. You boys make me feel quite alive again."

Charlotte's yellow boots came into the doorway and she said, "Don't be metaphoric at a time like this, Dick. These boys have obviously had quite a shock. Or two. Or maybe a dozen for all we know."

She set to coaxing Joaquin out from under the bed. I knew he'd be a sucker any minute. Sure enough, he started crawling out and even sat in her lap and let her hold him. Well, I wasn't going to cave for Richard whether he said he was Dead Uncle Dick or not.

But then Joaquin started talking with Charlotte. I could see how he'd gotten carried away with telling the truth the other day. It was just so easy for him to say it all to them. I perked up when Joaquin said, "If you're Dead Uncle Dick, are you going to tell us where you left the treasure?"

Charlotte answered instead. "Can you tell us more about this treasure of Dead Uncle Dick's?"

So then Joaquin launches into the whole thing. I was getting so mad at him I wanted to actually punch him. I regretted all the opportunities I'd had that I'd never taken.

Richard was laughing at some of the stuff he said, and that made me even madder. When Joaquin seemed to be finished spilling it all, he settled back into Charlotte's arms and Richard took another try at me. He said, "Okay, Cheyenne. I'll tell it like it is. You can believe me or not."

Well, that was fair, so I decided to listen.

"I'm Richard Walker, your uncle. This is my wife, Charlotte, your aunt. Those are our formal names. But our nicknames are Dick and Lotta."

I needed some time to think this through, but he was charging on.

"My younger brothers are Marc and Douglas and Brett. My younger sisters are Amy and Coco, who got very mad at Charlotte and me when we moved far away across the ocean to work in the Peace Corps. They thought we'd abandoned them. In a way I guess we had.

"Then Lotta and I took jobs with an organization that sent us out into countries with rough roads full of pot holes where the people hardly have any food and have to walk miles and miles just for water to drink. We felt like we were helping people who had no one to look after them. If we didn't do the job, who would? That's why we didn't come back to visit our family like we should have. When a person says someone is 'dead to them,' it often means they've been apart so long they don't know anything about each other. I'm sorry for that now.

"Our telephones usually didn't work, and we didn't get mail very often. We didn't know for months afterward that your momma was missing and that your grandma Walker had died. When we found out it made us very sad, but it seemed like the family back here had taken care of everything.

"Next thing we heard, you boys and your aunt Amy had disappeared. We became so worried that we left the poor people to fend for themselves and told the organization we worked for that we were going to retire. That means we planned to quit our jobs, leave. We knew we had made a big mistake staying away from our family for so long. We tried to come back quickly, but it took the organization awhile to find people who could replace us. We've come to help you."

I couldn't help myself. All this was like a truth potion. I said, "Uncle Marc says he's going to take us away from Aunt Amy. We're not going to let him."

Richard said, "Neither am I."

I had to think about this answer. There were several possibilities in my mind when he said, "Listen, Cheyenne, my bony bum is starting to hurt on this hard floor. Is there any chance you could come out from under the bed so we can talk over plans in a more comfortable setting?"

Plans. I needed one. Around the edges of my heart I could hear Richard saying that he and Charlotte really wanted us.

Then Charlotte said, "We're having toasted turkey sandwiches with warm tomato soup for lunch, and I made chocolate chip cookies especially for you."

I could feel myself melting inside. This was even worse than with Collette. My mind still hadn't decided, but my legs started crawling out on their own. I felt completely fractured as I tried to stand up.

And then Uncle Richard put his long arms around me and hugged me close. I started to cry and cry and cry like I had years of crying stored up inside me. I'd still be crying now except he said, "Actually, I've got a few treasures stored up especially to show a boy like you."

Then I started crying and laughing all together because I didn't have to be strong and brave anymore.

# THIRTY-SEVEN

# LKC

A nd that's pretty much how it's been ever since. We're all getting a little softer around the edges. Uncle Richard and Aunt Charlotte listen to our stories and laugh at our jokes, and we never think of getting paid. We are kids that don't need much money. Joaquin has baby fat again and nobody would ever think of me as a Stick Man. Aunt Amy is learning how to match up her ideas with words again, and Joaquin and I go to school every day.

I explained to Aunt Lotta about our food hoard in the book bags. She understood. When they were helping the poor people, if anything went wrong, there they'd be, babies crying, everybody sick, hungry as can be. I knew what she meant. She talked the problem over with Uncle Dick and they decided to keep a big supply of food that doesn't spoil for the whole family. That's us.

They also think it's a fine idea for Joaquin and me to keep our own food hoard in the back of our closets. That way everybody feels safe. Every three months we change it out. Joaquin and I haul out our old book bags and set everything on the kitchen counter. Then we shop from the cupboards and take what we want and put it in our book bags and hide it away again. I feel very comfortable with that arrangement.

I tell everyone at school to call me LKC. I never tell them what it means. But one evening while I was hosing down the front sidewalk I told Uncle Dick that it meant Lion King's Cub. He laughed and said he guessed that made him the Lion King. He'd always wanted to be a lion king and thanks for the chance.

## The End

# DISCUSSION QUESTIONS

1. Do you think that having a food hoard is something for all children to consider, or only children in an unstable family situation like Cheyenne and Joaquin?

2. How does Cheyenne's concept of family and his position within his family change and develop?

3. Why do you think Coco decided to leave her boys in Aunt Amy's care? If you were Cheyenne or Joaquin, would you think her reasons were good enough?

4. What do the boys learn from being sight dogs on grown-ups? How much difference is there between a dog and a wolf? Why does Grey Tooth think being a wolf will help him?

5. Cheyenne makes a lot of assumptions about Dead Uncle Dick. How does this influence the information Cheyenne hears about him later?

6. What do the initials LKC mean to Cheyenne and why does he feel so private about them?

7. What aspects of the Resilient Child do Cheyenne and Joaquin exhibit?

# ABOUT THE AUTHOR

Jean Stringam grew up in Alberta, Canada, taking three of her five degrees there, and remembers wonderful days riding horses, backpacking, and skiing with her family in the Canadian Rockies. Now that she lives far away from her five children and five sisters—located on both sides of the 49th parallel—she spends a lot of time travelling to see them. When they get together they love to make music, attend live theater, and hear each other's tales.

Nowadays she's either teaching for her university in Missouri or, better yet, she's teaching for them in a foreign country such as China or England. She loves to travel. If she had her way, she would visit every country in the world, including all the oceans, rivers, forests, and jungles. Whenever anyone asks her where home is, she thinks about all the people she has loved. If she could get them all together in one wonderful, happy pile, that would be home.